EVACUATION TO LOVE

Visit us at www.boldstrokesbooks.com

By the Author

Evacuation to Love

by

CA Popovich

2024

EVACUATION TO LOVE

ISBN 13: 978-1-63679-493-8

THIS TRADE PAPERBACK ORIGINAL IS PUBLISHED BY
BOLD STROKES BOOKS, INC.
P.O. BOX 249
VALLEY FALLS, NY 12185

FIRST EDITION: MARCH 2024

CREDITS
EDITOR: CINDY CRESAP
PRODUCTION DESIGN: SUSAN RAMUNDO
COVER DESIGN BY TAMMY SEIDICK

Dedication

To Love

CHAPTER ONE

Joanne Billings took a deep breath and whispered her final good-bye to the couple who had been her only parents. Joanne grew up in the foster care system and learned quickly not to develop close relationships because they never lasted. She grew to believe she couldn't count on anyone staying around and learned to take care of and keep to herself. Her final foster home came when she turned sixteen. She was an angry, self-destructive teen when Cindy and William Billings adopted her. For the first time in her life, she felt accepted and cared about. They gave her a last name along with a tiny hope for the future. They paid for her to attend community college and encouraged her to become a responsible adult. Despite being diagnosed with fetal alcohol syndrome, she finished a year of college and obtained a job as a teller at the local bank.

Depression and despair threatened as Joanne cleaned out her parents' apartment, and she sighed at the realization that she was completely alone in the world again. She was born an orphan and now she was one again. She gently set the urns containing their cremated remains on her dresser when she got home to her studio apartment in upper Michigan and flopped onto her back on her bed. There would be time after work tomorrow to go through the pile of papers in a large box she'd found next to her father's desk.

Joanne woke to bright sunlight shining into her bedroom and groaned as she realized she'd forgotten to set her alarm. She rose and set up her coffee maker before grabbing her phone and calling work. "Sorry, Bill. I'll be in late this morning," she said to her boss.

"No worries, Jo. Take the day off. I know it's hard to lose parents. Take tomorrow, too, if you need it."

"Thank you. I do have quite a bit more to do to clear out their apartment. I'll see you in a couple of days." She poured herself a cup of coffee and sat at her small kitchen table grateful for the extra time to settle their affairs. She made herself a bowl of oatmeal and finished breakfast before showering, dressing, and heading back to the apartment. It was dark by the time she finished sorting their belongings and packing the boxes she planned to take for donations. "I think that's everything, Mom and Pop." She swiped away tears and took one last look around the now empty apartment before locking the door and closing it behind her. Time to accept the loss and move on. She gently placed the small box of her mother's collector plates in the back seat of her car and the unopened bottle of her dad's aftershave next to it. They were all she planned to keep along with her memories of them.

Joanne grabbed a bottle of sparkling water when she got home and began sorting through the box of papers. She set aside several grocery store receipts and check stubs from rent payments. She filed away the title to their now demolished car and made a note to call the junk yard who'd towed it away. Feeling slightly overwhelmed, she set the rest of the paperwork aside and called her girlfriend.

"Hi, Joanne. You home now?"

"Yeah, Stacy. I have tomorrow off, too. Can you come over?"

"It depends. Are you still going to be all weepy and sad?"

Joanne sighed deeply. "They were my parents, Stace. I miss them."

"Yeah well, they're gone now. So move on. We'll go shopping at that new high-end fashion store tomorrow. That'll take your mind off them."

"I'm not interested in shopping. Can't we just cuddle on the couch and watch a movie?"

"Boring!"

"Okay. You come over and we can talk about it." Joanne cringed at Stacy's loud groan.

"I'll see you tomorrow," Stacy murmured before hanging up.

Joanne decided to finish sorting the rest of the papers the next day. Maybe Stacy would get bored and go shopping alone. Maybe she wouldn't even show up. She put the box on one of the empty shelves in her kitchen and went to bed.

Her alarm woke her in the middle of a dream in which she was seated in the back seat of her parents' station wagon. She smiled at the memory of the trip they'd taken to a small lake in Canada as she turned off her alarm and drifted in the feeling of love and acceptance. She'd accepted her limitations when her parents explained to her why she struggled with simple math problems and battled memory issues. Her birth mother had refused to give up her alcohol consumption while pregnant even at the doctor's insistence. It resulted in what the doctors called fetal alcohol syndrome in the fetus. Joanne had had to fight her whole life to learn basic skills and only after being adopted by her parents did she learn about her disability. They'd found a therapist who specialized in people with the disorder so Heather had been in her life for years. She pushed aside the anger at what she couldn't change and vowed to live up to her promise to her parents to continue her therapy. She got out of bed and poured a cup of coffee before retrieving the box of papers she'd set on the shelf and sorted them into two piles. She understood some of them were more important than others but planned to ask Heather for help with anything she didn't understand. The last folder in the box had her name and an address label on it. An address in Florida. She opened it and sorted through the contents and was surprised to come across a deed to a house. She turned it over several times before setting it aside and opening an envelope with her name on it. She gently withdrew a handwritten note and began to read.

If you're reading this, honey, it means we have gone to be with the Lord. Please don't feel alone, because Mom and I will be with you always. We are so proud of you and love you very much. All of our finances are at the same credit union as your account, and we know you will be taken care of and Heather will be there to help you sort out anything you don't understand. The house in Florida was originally a time-share but we never had much time to use it. We bought it in hopes of retiring there. It's yours now and we hope you will make use of it. Love, Dad.

Joanne wiped away tears and sat back in her chair. What in the world would she do with a house in Florida? How would she even get there was a bigger question. She put the note, deed, and insurance papers back into the folder and took it to her desk. The top middle drawer, labeled *Most Important*, held any paperwork she needed to keep. She sat for a moment as vague memories surfaced of the one long road trip when her parents had taken her to the Florida house. She tried to remember details, but it had been fifteen years ago. The rest of the papers in the box were receipts for paid bills and her mother's stamp collection. She never could figure out what her mother enjoyed about looking at all the numbers and pictures on the stamps. She put everything back into the box and set it back on the shelf before checking her phone for a message from Stacy. She wasn't surprised there wasn't one and ignored a feeling of sadness. She checked the time and called Heather.

Her therapist answered on the second ring. "Hi, Joanne. Everything okay?"

"I think so, Heather. I found a deed to a house in Florida among my parents' papers. I'm hoping you can help me figure out what to do with it." Joanne took two deep breaths to ground herself and concentrated on Heather's voice.

"Certainly. Do you want to come to my office?"

"Could you come here? I have tomorrow off work."

"No problem, kiddo. Ten a.m. okay with you?"

"Thank you. I'll see you tomorrow morning." Joanne put her phone on its charger and wrote the appointment on the ever-present notepad next to it. Then she called Stacy. She left a voice mail message explaining that she had an appointment the next morning and hoped that they could get together in the afternoon. She didn't hold out much hope that she'd get a response. Joanne returned to her parents' apartment to make sure she hadn't missed anything and vacuumed every room before putting the vacuum in her car and returning to the living room. She lay on her back in the middle of the room and stared at the ceiling waiting for the memories. Warmth flowed over her as she remembered her mother turning up the heat. She smiled at the memory of her father reminding her how high the utility bills could be. She imagined the scent of cooked chicken reminding her of the many meals they'd shared. So many memories she never wanted to lose. They were all she had left of the only adults in her life who'd cared about her. Who'd offered her a life beyond foster care. Seventeen years later, they were taken from her by a careless driver. An over-the-road trucker pushing for just a few more miles fell asleep at the wheel and changed her life forever. She rolled to her side and pushed herself up to her feet. She locked the door behind her before she headed to the office to turn in her parents' keys.

Joanne called Stacy as soon as she returned to her car. She left another message on her voice mail and hoped for a response soon. She took a deep breath and drove to her favorite spot next to a wooded area. She watched a white-tailed doe and her fawn graze for a few moments before she headed home.

CHAPTER TWO

S hanna Mills tossed the negative early result pregnancy test into the waste basket and wrestled with her conflicting feelings. Relief warred with disappointment. She hadn't told her husband about her missed period and now she didn't have to. Their seven-year marriage had settled into a convenient arrangement. He had a wife to accompany him to his law firm's obligatory functions, and she'd filled her obligation to her parents to appear heterosexual. Having grandchildren was their dream, but she had no great desire for the responsibility. The day she took her wedding vows and accepted her fate as arm candy for her attorney husband, she'd resigned herself to a life based on others' expectations. She smiled as she began to prepare homemade spaghetti sauce for dinner. She'd made it past another month and even though she and Paul hadn't been intimate for months, her relief encouraged her to begin taking the birth control pills she'd received from her doctor at her last appointment. She'd decide for herself when and if she wanted kids. Shanna checked the time and estimated her husband would be home in an hour. She turned the sauce to simmer and filled a pot with water for the noodles before pouring herself half a glass of wine and settling in her recliner for quiet time before he got home.

She went to turn on the stove to boil the water for noodles at the sound of his car pulling into the garage.

"I'm home, babe." He gave her a one-armed hug and a peck on her cheek. "Something smells great." He lifted the lid off the saucepan and sniffed.

"Dinner will be ready soon," Shanna said as she took the lid from him and stirred the sauce and was grateful when he turned away and left the room. She set the dining room table and put the pot of sauce in the middle with the noodles next to it. She sat in her usual chair and filled her plate while she waited for him to join her. Ten minutes later, he settled across from her and piled spaghetti on his plate.

"I need to go to a meeting tonight," he said between bites.

Shanna nodded, unsurprised by his statement. "Okay." She hoped it would be another night when he didn't come home. She had to make a change soon. How much longer could she fool herself into believing she was content with her life? It wasn't fair to her and it wasn't fair to her husband. Not that she believed he was unhappy with their arrangement, but they both could do better. She'd have to consider how much longer she could continue the sham. She finished her meal and put her dishes in the sink before turning to him. "Are you happy, Paul?" she asked.

He surprised her by getting up from the table and resting his hands on her hips. "I'm content." He squeezed her gently. "I know this is hard for you and I'll go along with whatever you need to do. We can divorce, but I'd ask you to please pretend for a couple more months. Just until I make partner. It shouldn't be longer than that."

"All right. I do wish the best for you, you know?"

"I do and I'm grateful." He kissed her cheek and left the room.

Shanna cleaned up the kitchen and loaded the dishwasher before pouring herself another half glass of wine and settling on the couch to call her mom.

"Hi, Shanna. Is everything okay?"

"Sure, Mom. I just wanted to hear your voice. How's everything in Florida?"

"Quiet and hot. I'm staying in and watching TV."

"I heard rumblings of a possible hurricane threat. Have you heard anything?"

"Not anything definite. It's the time of year for them though. How's Paul?"

"He's good. We just finished dinner and he's on his way back to work."

"Nothing new, huh?"

"Nope. But it's okay. We had a talk tonight."

"I'm glad, honey. Make the most of it with him."

"I am. I've got a pile of manuals to edit this week, so I'm keeping busy."

"Weren't you planning a week off?"

"Next week. I'm looking forward to the break."

"Well, pace yourself and you'll get through it, honey."

"I will. Thanks, Mom."

"Take care and we'll talk next week."

Shanna disconnected the call and went back to work. She finished two hours later, changed into her pajamas, and reclined in bed to read. She awoke to movement next to her on the bed an hour later. She hadn't expected Paul home until morning, and she lay as still as she could feigning sleep. To her relief, he didn't reach for her. She stayed as still as possible until sleep overtook her and woke alone to morning sunshine filtering into the room. She got up and put on her robe before going to the kitchen. Paul wasn't anywhere in the house and hadn't left a note so she presumed he was at work. She made herself a cup of coffee and took it to her screened-in porch overlooking the backyard. She enjoyed the view and peace and quiet while she ate a bowl of oatmeal and finished her coffee before dressing and returning to work. She worked for half an hour before rising to get another cup of coffee and turning on her TV to a news station. She turned up the volume when a weather alert warned of *conditions right for development of hurricanes.* She called her mother.

"Hello again, dear. Is everything okay?"

"I just heard a weather report regarding hurricanes and wanted to remind you to keep a close eye on the news." Shanna knew her mom loved living in Florida but was nervous about storms.

"Thank you, honey, but I'm not scared. I'll pay attention. They're watching development of possibly a big one, so I've got my television tuned to the weather channel."

"Okay, Mom. I'll let you be. Take care." Shanna disconnected the call and reminded herself her mother and father had lived in Florida for years before his death. Her mother could take care of herself. She finished reviewing her latest edits and closed her laptop. She poured herself another cup of coffee and took it to her favorite chair at her small drafting table, picked up her sketching pad and pencil, and began drawing. She lost herself in her task and relaxed into a rhythm. Half an hour later, she checked the time, stood to stretch, and refilled her coffee cup before she returned to her seat and reviewed her work. She usually drew what she saw outside the window. A dogwood tree covered in a thin layer of snow in the winter which she noted would be coming soon. Today it was in the last of its yearly blooms and she picked a few colored pencils to match the pinks and creamy whites. She lifted the finished product and chose a spot on one of the walls to display it. Paul considered her time creating artwork a waste of time, but to her it was soothing. An outlet for her creative side. Her work as an editor for automotive manuals gave her a sense of purpose and an income. But time spent creating a beautiful sketch was relaxing. It balanced her. She put away her supplies and went to take a shower.

Shanna poured herself a glass of iced tea before she settled at her desk to finish another manual. She considered options for dinner and decided on leftover spaghetti. Paul may or may not be home and she never minded leftovers. She finished eating, left the covered pot of sauce on the stove for Paul in case he came home, and went to work on her next art project. She checked the time an hour later and noted that Paul still wasn't home. She put the pot of spaghetti sauce in the refrigerator. Paul would find it if he was hungry. She changed into her pajamas, chose one of her romance novels, and settled in bed to read. Her mind kept diverting her to thoughts of Paul and why she kept up the pretense of their marriage. She loved reading romance but knew real life could never match the perfection of the novels. Maybe it was time for a change. Paul had offered her an out, and she began to think it would be the best for both of them. She'd have a talk with him when he got home. If he came home. She woke the next morning alone with her book next to her and her wine glass untouched on her nightstand. She rose and put on her robe before heading to the kitchen and putting a coffee pod in the Keurig. She reached for a coffee cup and noticed the envelope with her name on it propped against the wall next to it. She pulled the note from the envelope and began to read.

My dear Shanna. I can no longer continue this farce of a marriage. I've found someone who wants me for me. I've been offered full partnership in my firm and I need to move on. I believe it would be best for you, too. Take care. Paul

Shanna took the note to her desk, put it in the top drawer, slid it closed, and went back to work.

CHAPTER THREE

Joanne settled into a chair at her kitchen table to review all the information Heather had given her. Her head was spinning from the volume of data as she separated the papers into piles. She reviewed the folders Heather had helped her create and filed the piles away into the corresponding ones. When she finished, she sorted the folders alphabetically and put them into a file box. She sat quietly for a few moments staring at the file box holding her parents' life. She struggled to absorb the huge change in her life and what she would do next. She'd discussed the possibility of traveling to Florida with Heather and quickly became overwhelmed. It seemed so far away from everything she knew. She put the file box on the top shelf of her bedroom closet and stretched out on her bed. She rose after an hour and put a frozen macaroni and cheese into the oven. Stacy hadn't called or come over so she settled on her couch and looked up the address in Florida of what was now her house. Her phone displayed a picture of the small home on a street with several others. She liked the idea of an attached carport, but couldn't imagine how she'd find her way around the strange area. It'd taken her months to be comfortable knowing how to find her way in her small town in upper Michigan. She sighed and checked her phone for a message from Stacy but wasn't surprised there wasn't one. She rose and brought her meal to eat while she watched TV. Heather had told her she didn't need to make any decisions about Florida or anything else right away, but Joanne couldn't turn off her racing thoughts. So many unknowns confused and scared her.

One thing she knew for sure was that she was alone now.

She had Heather, but Heather had a life with her family. Joanne called Stacy and left a message when she didn't answer. She set her phone on her nightstand and let her tears fall into her pillow. She dragged herself off the bed and went to the kitchen to wash her dishes and get a glass of milk before she settled on her couch and watched the news on TV. Her phone interrupted her thoughts, but she smiled at the readout. Stacy finally called her back. "Hi, Stace. Thanks for getting back to me."

"I just got home from the store and got your message. Are you doing okay?"

"I am. Heather came over today and helped me sort some papers." Joanne wanted to say more but wasn't sure what else to say.

"Good. So, do you still want to go shopping with me?"

"I never wanted to go shopping, Stacy. I'm trying to figure out what to do next. Do you understand?"

"No. But it doesn't matter. We'll have fun."

"Stacy. I can't afford to go shopping. I have to figure out my finances and what I'm going to do next."

"What do you mean? Why do you have to do anything?"

For some reason, Joanne didn't want to share her new ownership of a house in Florida with Stacy. "I just don't know. I feel sort of lost, but I'll be okay."

"Good. I'll give you a call tomorrow maybe."

Joanne heard the click of Stacy's phone disconnecting and ended the call. She sighed realizing she needed to assess her relationship with Stacy. She retrieved her laptop, connected to the Internet, and typed in the address of her new house in Florida. She zoomed in on a couple of the homes in the neighborhood and liked what she saw. She decided to contact Heather and get her opinion on possibly visiting the area. She sent her a text and continued her search of Fort Meyers, Florida. Her research was interrupted by a response from Heather. She put her computer away and prepared her coffee maker for when she arrived.

"Thanks for coming over, Heather. I made coffee." Joanne poured two cups of coffee and set one next to Heather's right hand.

"Thank you." Heather took a sip and set the cup down. "What do you want to talk about?"

Joanne took a minute to organize her thoughts. "I looked up the Florida house my parents left me. I'd like to go check it out, and I hoped you could help me do that."

"I can see why you would want to, Joanne." She took a deep breath. "I'll look into flights for next week. Is that okay with you?"

"Thank you, Heather!"

Heather stood and wrapped her arms around Joanne in a hug. "Make sure you have any paperwork regarding that house. And bring any keys you find." She kissed her cheek before leaving.

Joanne wrote herself a note to look for keys and put it next to the deed. She wrote another note to remind herself to let her boss know when she'd be gone. She missed her parents terribly, but knowing she'd find a place where they'd spent time comforted her a lot. She went to her bedroom closet and began to sort clothes. From the research she'd done, she learned it was hot and humid in Florida so she pulled out two pair of shorts from her dresser along with a few T-shirts and her bathing suit. She retrieved her suitcase from under her bed and wished that her parents had taken her to their Florida house more than once. Her dad's note sounded like they'd had it for several years, but she didn't know what to expect. Hopefully, she'd get an answer when she and Heather went there. She went back to searching for information on Fort Meyers, Florida.

Joanne put her computer away and gathered all the information she had from her parents' box of papers. Her dad's note said they wanted to retire there, and tears formed at the thought of all their future plans being destroyed by a careless driver. She'd go see the house for herself and decide what to do with it then. She put all the information regarding the house in a pile on her kitchen table and filed away the rest of the papers.

The next day, Joanne let her boss know she'd be gone for a few days to settle her parents' affairs. She had all the information she could find on the Florida house in a folder ready to take with her and the closer their day of departure came, the more excited she became. Heather had made the flight arraignment so all she had to do was be packed and ready to leave. She looked forward to her first time on an airplane and was grateful for Heather in her life to help her navigate the trip. She called Stacy to let her know when she'd be gone and got her voice mail. She'd either get the message she left or not, and Joanne realized it didn't matter if she didn't.

Stacy would take care of Stacy. Joanne felt her life taking an important turn, and she doubted very much that Stacy would want to be part of it or that she even wanted her to be. She allowed herself a moment of sadness, then took a deep breath and marked the time and flight number Heather had given her on the large calendar she kept on the front of her refrigerator.

"Ready to go, Jo?" Heather called from the doorway when she arrived on their day of departure.

"I am." Joanne rolled her suitcase behind her and carried her backpack. "I'm excited, but a little nervous."

"Nothing to be nervous about. Think of it as an adventure." Heather loaded her suitcase into the car.

Joanne never could have imagined what flying would be like, and she found herself fascinated as the plane rose into the sky and the ground grew farther away. "This is amazing," she murmured.

"I thought you'd like it," Heather replied, grinning. "I love flying."

The flight was over too soon for Joanne, but she did look forward to finding the house that now belonged to her. She followed Heather and the planeload of people off the plane into the air-conditioned terminal. She kept her nerves at bay by staying close to Heather, and soon they had their luggage and were standing outside the terminal waiting for a taxi in the Florida heat and humidity. "Wow. It's hot here."

"We'll get a taxi soon, Jo. I hope your parents put air conditioning in that house of yours."

Joanne hoped so, too as she wiped the sweat off her forehead with her sleeve. She followed Heather into the back seat of the taxi when it arrived and took a deep breath as she gave the driver the address to her house. The driver pulled into a paved driveway and parked in the carport forty-five minutes later. Joanne climbed out of the back seat and rushed to the door to try the key she'd found in an envelope labeled *Florida house*. To her surprise, the door wasn't locked. Her parents wouldn't have left the house unlocked. Would they? She stepped through the door and stepped over a pile of clothes. The kitchen sink was full of unwashed dishes and a pot of water sat on a burner of the stove. Something was definitely off. She knew her parents hadn't been there, and she turned to Heather who shrugged.

"Let's lock the door now and check out the rest of the house," Heather said as she strode to the living room. "Oh, my!"

CHAPTER FOUR

Shanna sat at her drafting table and stared out the window. She hadn't expected to feel loneliness if Paul ever left, but she had to admit what she felt. They'd agreed from the beginning that theirs would be a marriage of convenience. She'd played her part for appearances as his wife, and they'd settled into a comfortable life. She'd convinced herself that love was for other people and she could live without it. The emptiness in her heart would fade eventually. She lost herself in another drawing until the sun set and the room darkened. She changed and went to bed where she tossed and turned and finally gave up. She rose to make herself a cup of tea and settled on her couch to consider how her life would change. The house was in both their names, but it was paid for. She picked up a pad of paper and pencil and began a list. Paul would probably stop by to pick up his clothes and they could talk then. She hoped he wouldn't insist she buy him out, but they could probably agree on a payment plan. She pushed aside her jumbled thoughts and went back to bed.

The next morning, Shanna wrote a note for Paul letting him know she wanted to talk. His note sounded like he'd probably move out, but she wanted clarification. The house was close to the grocery where she shopped, and the room she'd set up for her artwork was perfect, so she didn't want to move. She focused on her next manual for work and left the note for Paul on the kitchen counter.

Shanna arrived home from the store that afternoon to find all of Paul's clothes gone along with their small dining room table and chairs, the couch, and the microwave. "What the hell?" she mumbled. She checked the bedroom and was grateful he hadn't taken the bed. She checked the rest of the house and sighed with relief that her art studio hadn't been touched. Maybe she wouldn't get a chance to talk to him after all. She heated leftovers for dinner and settled into her recliner to eat while she considered her situation. She hadn't thought that Paul would've just left without a good-bye, but it seemed as if he was gone. She finished eating and got his voice mail when she called his cell. She took a deep breath to calm herself before leaving a good-bye message. She wished she could change the locks, but he still co-owned the house. Her next call was to her mother.

"Hello, dear. Is everything okay? You don't usually call this late," her mother said.

"I just wanted to say hello and see how you were doing." Shanna made herself a cup of tea while she spoke.

"I'm fine, but you sound a little off."

"Paul left me today. I'm not surprised by it, but he took our couch."

"Ah. Couches are replaceable, honey. Did you two have a fight?"

"No. He found someone he liked better than me and left for her." Shanna sipped her tea realizing it didn't hurt too much to tell her mom about Paul.

"I'm sorry you're going through that, honey. I thought maybe you two were working things out and getting closer. Can I help in any way? Would you like to come stay with me for awhile?"

"Thanks, Mom, but I'll be okay. We didn't have a very close relationship anyway, so maybe this is for the best." Shanna took a breath and realized the truth of her statement.

"Do you need me to come there? I can leave right away."

"No, thank you. I'll be fine, but I'd love to have you visit whenever you want to."

"Okay. You try to relax and let me know if you need anything."

"I will. Thanks, Mom." Shanna disconnected the call and finished her tea before going to start another sketch. Twenty minutes later, she realized her art wasn't relaxing her as it usually did. She was distracted and slightly unsettled, so she took a deep breath and focused on what she wanted to do next. Her mother lived five hundred miles away so it wasn't like she could just pop over for a visit, but it was comforting to talk to her. Paul may or may not come back to the house, but they'd have to talk about finances eventually. She went back to working on her artwork and pushed aside thoughts of Paul and his new life. She worked for an hour before she went to bed.

Shanna startled awake when the bedroom door opened and Paul walked into the room. "What are you doing here?" She stepped out of bed and put on her robe.

"I wanted to talk about us."

"You made it pretty clear that there is no *us* Paul. *You* have no right and are unwanted here. Go back to your girlfriend."

"I'll leave if that's what you want, but we need to talk."

"It is what I want. I'll file for divorce tomorrow. You'll be free."

"Fine. I did only want to say good-bye, Shanna. I didn't mean to upset you. Take my name off the house on the divorce settlement. You keep it. We'll work out the bank account next week." He turned and left.

Shanna locked the door behind him with shaky hands and took a deep breath. Paul's unexpected late-night visit unnerved her. She shivered and pulled her robe tightly around her. The morning couldn't come soon enough to get to the divorce attorney. She made herself a cup of tea and dropped into her recliner to settle her nerves before heading back to bed.

The meeting with her attorney the next day didn't take long, and he assured her that the divorce papers would be served to Paul within the week. She left his office confident that their marriage would be dissolved soon, and they could both move on. She finished her work for the day and struggled to relax. She couldn't understand what had happened with Paul and their amenable agreement. It seemed as if this new woman in his life was a significant influence. She changed the locks on the doors with the ones she picked up on her way home. Paul could call if he needed anything and if he was ready to settle their finances. She reflected on his odd behavior as she finished dinner and settled at her drafting table to finish the project she'd started the day before. She found herself too distracted, so she put her work aside and turned on the television. She turned off the TV after the nightly news and went to bed.

Shanna woke to pounding on the front door. Her first thought was that it was Paul. She put on her robe and opened the door. "Now what?" She stood with the door open but blocking the entrance.

"I want to apologize for bursting in on you yesterday. It wasn't fair to you. I've made partner, so I want to settle our finances and let you move on." He handed her a folder full of papers. "I removed my name from all our accounts except the one at my company credit union. I'll be moving to California next month, so you'll be rid of me." Paul stood still as he spoke.

"Okay. Thank you, Paul. I appreciate it. I just filed the divorce papers. I'd appreciate it if you signed them before you go out of state."

"I will, Shanna. Again, I'm sorry for scaring you. Be well." Paul began to reach for her but dropped his hand half-way, turned, and walked away.

Shanna closed and locked the door with a feeling of relief mixed with sadness. She hoped he'd find happiness with his new woman. She made herself a sandwich and settled in her recliner to eat and go through the papers he left her. Satisfied that things were in order, and she'd be financially secure, she set the folder aside and called her mother.

"Hello, dear," her mother answered.

"Hi, Mom. I wanted to say hello and let you know that Paul and I are getting divorced."

"I'm sorry to hear that, honey. Are you all right?"

"I am, Mom. Paul made partner at his firm and is moving to California. I think it's to be with someone else. I do wish him happiness."

"You take care of yourself and let me know if I can do anything. Living alone will be an adjustment for you. I remembered how I felt when your father died. It was tragic and heartbreaking and, besides the loss, a life-changing event for me. I hope you have friends you can turn to. Please let me know if I can do anything. I can get a flight and be there tomorrow if you need me, honey."

"I'll let you know, Mom, and I appreciate it." Shanna disconnected the call and filed away the papers before logging on to her computer to look for a couch. She arranged for delivery and shut down her computer before she made herself a cup of tea and sank into her recliner to read. Her mind began to wander within a few minutes. She and Paul had presented themselves to her mother as a happy couple when they'd married. Now that he was gone, she deliberated telling her mom she hoped to find a woman to live with her. She didn't regret the few years she'd spent with Paul, but the totally unfulfilling relationship had taken its toll. She had gotten so good at pretending to the world, she wasn't sure she knew how to be in an honest relationship. She sighed. It probably wouldn't happen anyway. She set her book aside and went to get ready for bed. Tomorrow would be soon enough to figure out the rest of her life.

CHAPTER FIVE

W hat is it, Heather?" Joanne took in the room and realized what had prompted Heather's remark. It was obvious someone had been sleeping on the couch, and the small coffee table was covered with empty take-out food containers. The floor was littered with wrappers, and the scent of cigarette smoke lingered in the air. "Someone's living here!"

"It looks like it, Joanne. Florida has squatter's rights laws. We'll have to find out how long they've been here and work to get them out."

"Squatters? What does that mean?"

"People can move into, and live in, a vacant property in Florida. The scary part is that if they've been here seven years they can claim it as their own."

Joanne swallowed the panic rising in her throat. Would she lose this house before she even had it? "How can we find out?"

"I'm not sure." Joanne followed Heather through the house and looked into each room. "The bedrooms look unused and don't appear to be any toiletries in the bathroom. I'm hoping it means whoever slept here hasn't been here long. We'll change the locks and add dead bolts before we leave. Hopefully, that will be enough to keep them out." They went out to the carport and checked the area for any sign someone had been there. Joanne found two folding chairs and opened them for them to sit.

"Hello?" A gray-haired woman waved as she crossed the street and approached them. "I'm Betty Walters. I live across the street." She pointed to her house and continued to walk into the carport.

Joanne stood to greet her. "Hello."

"You must be the Billings girl. I met your mom and dad a few years ago. Are they with you?"

"No." Joanne took a deep breath before continuing. "They passed away last month. A car accident."

"I'm so sorry. I didn't know them well, but I'm so sorry for your loss." Betty looked like she was going to pull her into a hug but stepped back.

Heather stood to introduce herself. "My name's Heather. I'm a friend of the family and helped Joanne come to check on the house. Have you seen squatters here?"

"I have. They moved in last week. I hope they haven't trashed the place."

"I think we got lucky. They haven't done any damage that we can see."

"Good. I worried about it, but all I could do was call the police. Are you moving in now?" she asked Joanne.

"I…I'm not sure what I'm going to do." Joanne hadn't thought about keeping the house. It seemed like a huge responsibility living so far away. "I'm glad we could come and check on it."

"If you have time, stop by for a cup of coffee or something." Betty smiled and turned to go home.

"Shall we go back in and check all the rooms?" Heather stood and reached for Joanne's hand.

"Yeah. I'd like to see if Mom and Dad left anything here." Joanne followed Heather as they checked each room. She was glad the only evidence of the squatter was in the living room. "It looks like everything is okay." She wasn't surprised that her parents hadn't left anything personal in the house since they never spent much time there, but she took a deep breath, closed her eyes, and imagined she felt their arms around her in a loving hug.

"We'd better call a cab so we can get some groceries. I'll call while you take an inventory of the fridge and cupboards." Heather made the call.

An hour later, they returned with food and Joanne began the search for bedding while Heather made a huge salad. "I found it!" She held up an armload of sheets, pillowcases, and blankets. She removed all the bedding from the couch, pleased to find a stackable washer/dryer she could use to wash them. "It's sort of nice here, isn't it?" Joanne asked as they sat on the couch to eat.

"It is," Heather replied. "Your parents did good buying this house. It's in a nice quiet neighborhood, but still close enough to the water."

"We have four days, right?" Joanne asked.

"Yes. We're scheduled to fly back on Sunday."

"Can we take a ride to the water tomorrow? I'd love to see how close we are."

"I think that's a great idea. Shall we see if this little TV works?" Heather clicked the remote and found the television tuned in to a news channel.

Joanne relaxed after dinner and wondered if her parents had sat on this couch watching the same television. She enjoyed the feeling of closeness to them. "I feel like my parents are here with us. Does that make any sense, Heather?"

"Of course it does, Joanne. You just lost them and we're here where they'd spent time. I think they'd be very happy and proud that you made it to this house."

"I'm going to keep it." Joanne rested her head on the back of the couch and scanned the ceiling as she imagined her mom and dad sitting cuddled together. "I'm definitely going to keep it."

"I think that's a fine idea." Heather squeezed her hand.

"Hello?"

Joanne heard someone calling from the door. She immediately thought of the squatters and prepared herself to send them away. She opened the door to her neighbor, Betty.

"Sorry to intrude, but I baked a Bundt cake this afternoon, and I thought it would be neighborly to share it with you."

"Please, come in," Joanne said as Heather came into the room.

"We have Bundt cake!" Joanne grinned as she carried it to the kitchen counter. "Have a seat, on the couch, Betty. We were just watching the news." She cut three pieces of cake, placed them on small plates, and carried them to the living room. She smiled at the feeling of rightness. Like she was entertaining in her own home.

"This is nice. No wonder the squatters broke in here," Betty said and smiled.

"It is nice. I didn't remember that my parents owned a house in Florida until I found the deed in their papers. They'd only brought me here once when I was seventeen."

"Again, I'm sorry for your loss, Joanne."

"Thank you. I miss them. I always will." Joanne smiled sadly.

"Well, I'm glad you made it here so I could meet you. I have a daughter your age. She and her husband live in South Carolina." Betty took a bite of cake.

"How long have you lived here, Betty?" Heather asked.

"Jim and I settled in our house over twenty years ago. He had a fatal heart attack three years ago. I still miss him terribly."

"I'm sorry, Betty. It's hard to lose loved ones. I know that firsthand now," Joanne said as she swiped away a tear.

"So, how long are you two staying?" Betty asked.

"We fly home on Sunday." Joanne took a bite of cake.

"I hope you'll come back, Joanne. It's a safe neighborhood."

"We'll see. I have a job in Michigan and an apartment." Joanne didn't mention her girlfriend. Stacy probably wouldn't miss her if she left anyway.

"I think it'll be nice for Joanne to have this place to visit," Heather said.

"I hope you'll come back with me," Joanne declared.

"Anytime," Heather replied, smiling.

"Well, I'm going to head home and leave you two alone." Betty stood and hugged Joanne. "I'm glad to meet you and hope to see you again soon."

Joanne walked Betty to the door and locked it after she left. She hoped she'd see Betty again, too. She reclaimed her seat on the couch and took a few minutes to gather her thoughts. "It is a nice house isn't it, Heather?"

"Yes. It is. What're you thinking, Joanne?"

"If I keep it, I'll have to figure out how to keep squatters away. What if I moved here?" She waited for Heather's objection.

"Is that what you're thinking about doing?"

"Maybe. It's a big move though. I could live for a while with what Mom and Dad left me." She considered the effort it would take to move over a thousand miles away. "If I do, would you help me?"

"Of course I would. But promise me you'll think about it a while. Make a list of positives and negatives like I showed you when you moved to your apartment." Heather squeezed her hand and smiled.

"I will. I really like it here." Joanne counted it her first positive.

❖

"I can't believe it's time to go home already," Joanne said as she finished packing her suitcase. They'd spent time at the beach and went to dinner at Betty's twice.

"It has been nice. Just remember that visiting is very different than living here. Don't forget that if you make the decision to move," Heather said.

"I will. Maybe I need to visit again before deciding." Joanne finished cleaning the kitchen and walked through the house before carrying her suitcase to the door. "The cab is here," she called to Heather as she took one last look around the room. She'd have a lot to think about and plan if she decided to make the move. She turned her thoughts to the upcoming flight home.

CHAPTER SIX

Shanna stretched out on her new couch to read and enjoy her newfound feeling of freedom. Freedom to be who she was and live free of pretense. She didn't know what came next in her life, but she knew it wouldn't be another husband. Her mother would have to accept her for who she was and who she loved. She picked up her phone and called her mom.

"Hi, honey."

"Hi, Mom. I'm relaxing on my new couch, and I thought I'd call to see how you were doing."

"I'm fine. I met a new neighbor last week. She's your age and just lost her parents."

"That's hard. I'm glad you were able to visit her."

"So, you have a new couch, and is Paul still around?"

"No. We said our good-byes and he's off to California. He ended up being fair about things. I have the house now. I'm not certain what will be next in my life, but I know it won't be living with a man."

"I'm glad you're going to be okay, dear, no matter who you decide to live with next. I just want to see you happy. Let me know if you need anything. I can come there if you're lonely. Life is too short to live with loneliness."

"Thanks, Mom, but I'll be fine. Take care." Shanna disconnected the call and went back to her book. Her reading was interrupted by her phone. "Hello?"

"Hi, Shanna. It's Paul. I just wanted to let you know I arrived safely. I hope you are well."

"I'm good. Thanks, Paul, and I hope you settle in there."

"I have and I found I like the weather."

"You have a good life, Paul. Good-bye." Shanna disconnected the call. She had no desire to keep in touch with him and hoped he wouldn't call again. She went back to reading.

The next morning, Shanna made herself breakfast and began work without a thought of Paul. She knew it would be different without him, and she sighed in relief. She'd replaced the door locks after he left with locks and dead bolts with different keys. She needed two keys to get in and felt a little silly at her obsessiveness, but she felt secure in keeping Paul out in case he returned. She considered her mom alone in another state and herself alone now. She picked up her phone and called her mother.

"Hello, honey."

"Hi, Mom. I just wanted to check in with you. Are you doing okay?"

"I am. I just visited my new neighbor across the street. Her parents left her the house and she's there with a friend."

"Is she planning to stay there?"

"I don't know for sure. I sort of hope she does. It would be nice to have someone younger in the neighborhood."

"Is your offer to come here for a visit still good?"

"Absolutely. It takes some getting used to living alone after years of company. Even if you and Paul weren't close toward the end."

"Yeah. Let me know when you're ready to leave. I'll put the coffee on." Shanna smiled. Her mother loved her coffee. She disconnected the call and went to her garage to look for paint. It was time to make her house hers. She took inventory of the paint containers and returned to the kitchen with one. She chose beige and planned to trim around the windows with white. It took her three hours to finish and step back to review her work. In a few days, the house would be totally the way she wanted it.

She finished cleaning up in the kitchen and decided to tackle her mother's room next. She chose pale yellow for the walls. Her mom's favorite color. She looked the room over after she was done and made a note to shop for new bedding. Her mother would love a fluffy down comforter and cotton sheets. She cleaned her brushes and put them away with the paint. The next room she'd work on would be her bedroom. Paul had chosen the blue color and she'd gone along with it. By tomorrow it would be light sea foam green. Her favorite color.

Shanna stood in the middle of the third bedroom unable to decide on a color. It had white walls and a beautiful maroon comforter on the double bed. She decided it would be fine if she ever had an overnight visitor and it would be enough work finishing the other rooms. She went to the kitchen to make herself a sandwich and bowl of soup.

The next morning, she woke to the scent of paint. She rose and opened a window in her mom's room before she scrambled eggs for breakfast and relaxed on her couch to drink a cup of coffee and eat. She took a deep breath and enjoyed relaxing in her own home without the stress of Paul's energy. She began a shopping list for what she'd cook when her mother came to visit and decided to finish painting her bedroom before heading to take a shower.

Shanna stood in the doorway of her bedroom and admired the newly painted room. She'd put up with the blue Paul had insisted on for years. Now it felt like her room. Maybe she'd get herself a new comforter, too. She put away all her painting supplies and returned to her couch to enjoy the sense of serenity. Her painting efforts had taken most of the day, but she considered the work well worth it. She felt herself beginning to claim the house as her own and recognized a feeling of rightness. And security.

She took a cup of coffee with her to her art studio and worked on a new drawing until the daylight began to fade. She realized it had been a long time since she'd been able to completely relax into her artwork so intensely to lose track of time. She rose to make dinner and checked the kitchen clock to estimate how long before

Paul was due home. She'd begun purging him from the house, but it seemed it would take a little longer to purge him from her memory. She warmed the last of the spaghetti sauce and ate before changing her clothes, grabbing a jacket, and heading out the door.

Shanna pulled into the nightclub's parking lot half an hour later and took a deep breath before exiting her car. It had been years since she'd allowed herself the freedom to visit the bar, and she hoped it still catered to a lesbian crowd after seven o'clock. She breathed a sigh of relief when she stepped through the door and handed a very attractive butch her cover charge. She squeezed past a few women dancing as she wound her way to the bar and ordered a beer. The long day of painting walls was catching up to her, so she took a seat at one of the empty small tables and enjoyed the feeling of freedom to toss aside the charade of her life. Shanna relaxed in her seat while she watched the dancers and sipped her beer. She smiled at the woman who approached her and settled in the chair across from her.

"Hello. I haven't seen you here before," she said. "I'm Barb. Can I buy you another beer?"

"Thanks, I'm Shanna." She finished the last swallow from her beer bottle and set it aside. "And I'd love another beer." She waited while Barb retrieved two fresh beers and returned to the table.

"Thank you." Shanna sipped her new beer. It was cold and refreshing and she forced herself to set the bottle down instead of gulping the contents.

"Would you dance with me?" Barb asked.

"Absolutely." Shanna stood and took Barb's outstretched hand. A huge sigh escaped unbidden the moment their bodies met. She'd longed for the feel of another woman in her arms for so long she thought she'd never experience it again. She followed Barb's lead and they swayed to the music. A fast song began, and they moved apart to dance as if they'd been doing it for years. "Thank you for the dance and the company tonight, Barb. I enjoyed it very much." Shanna finished her drink, stood, and took Barb's hand as she spoke.

"I've enjoyed it, too. I hope I see you here again," Barb breathed as she placed a gentle kiss on her lips.

Shanna nearly swooned and took a step back. "It's been a long time since I've been here, but I think I'll try to make it a regular event now. Thanks again." She squeezed Barb's hand and turned to leave. She replayed the evening in her mind as she drove home. Despite her attraction to women, there was the pressure from her parents to marry and settle down with a husband and children. She'd spent years denying her feelings and living the life expected of her. Now she wondered if she had the courage to live the life she wanted to. She shook off her musings and got ready for bed. She could sort out her feelings in the morning.

Shanna woke to her alarm and lay still for a few moments to allow memories of her evening at the club before getting up and turning her thoughts to work.

CHAPTER SEVEN

Joanne studied the US map she'd picked up at the bookstore. It was over a thousand miles between Michigan and Florida, and the thought of making that drive overwhelmed her. If she made the decision to move, she'd ask Heather for help. She'd offered to ride there with her and fly home so she'd have her car, and that seemed like a good plan. Starting a new life away from everything she knew felt daunting, but a sliver of excitement pushed its way through. She'd had her parents to lean on for help since she was sixteen. She'd carry the memories with her forever, but it was time to begin taking care of herself and taking control of her future. She reviewed the map and made her decision. She'd talk to Heather in the morning and ask her to help plan their road trip. She opened her closet door and began sorting her clothes. Before getting far, she made the decision to take them all with her and decide what she needed once she got there. She pulled out her suitcases and realized she'd need a few more. She could shop the next day after reviewing the few items other than clothes she would take. She went to bed with thoughts bouncing between leaving the life she knew and the adventure of starting a new one.

The next morning, she woke with a feeling of excitement. Her life was about to change and she looked forward to it. She dressed for work and mentally rehearsed how she would tell her boss she was leaving. She finished her workday and called Heather as soon as she got home.

"Hi, Jo. What's up?"

"I gave my notice at work today, Heather. I hope we can choose a day to leave for Florida."

"I have clients all this week," she said quietly. "Next week is totally open so far. Will that work for you?"

"I'll make it happen." Joanne grinned, excitement growing.

"Okay. Plan on a three-day drive. I'll help you make a list if you need me to."

"I think I'm okay. I have my clothes sorted, but I need to buy a couple more suitcases. Would it work for you if we left Wednesday?"

"Sounds good. I'll plan to spend the weekend with you if that's okay."

"Great!" Joanne smiled. She relaxed knowing she'd have help with the transition. She made a list of items she'd get for their trip and went shopping for suitcases.

The day before they were scheduled to leave, Joanne made sandwiches and packed bottled water and orange juice in insulated bags for the trip. She lined up her packed suitcases by the door before taking her car to fill it with gas. She was ready to embark on her new life adventure. She had one last call to make and she dialed Stacy's number.

"Hi, Joanne. What's up?" Stacy sounded bored.

"I wanted to let you know I'm moving to Florida. I'll send you the address, and I hope you'll come to visit someday."

"Florida? That house your parents left you?"

"Yes. It's nice. I think I'll be comfortable there."

"They have scorpions and alligators in Florida. Be careful and good luck. Have a nice life." Stacy disconnected the call.

Joanne wasn't surprised by Stacy's withdrawal, but it hurt. She took a deep breath and concentrated on her future plans. She loaded her suitcases into her car and drove to work to pick up her final paycheck. She hugged her boss good-bye and thanked him for his referral letter. She could begin a new job at the Florida branch of the bank where she'd worked as soon as she arrived. She pulled into Heather's driveway and loaded her suitcase into her car before they headed for the expressway.

"Thank you for coming with me, Heather." Joanne didn't take her eyes off the road as she spoke.

"I'm glad to. It's a nice getaway for me. My clients can get in touch with me by phone if they need me."

"I'm a little nervous, but I think I'm doing the right thing. The house would sit vacant and probably house squatters if I don't live there. I thought of something else, too." Joanne hesitated.

"What, Jo?" Heather rested her fingers lightly on her leg.

"I can always move back if I have to. Right?"

"Absolutely. And don't forget you can call me anytime. I'll always be here for you."

Joanne took a deep breath and concentrated on driving.

"Is Stacy going to visit sometime?"

"Huh." Joanne shook her head. "No. She, well, she's not interested in Florida. Or me, apparently."

"I'm sorry, Jo. You deserve to find someone who cares about you. Maybe you'll find her in Florida."

Joanne drove and focused on the route. She'd think about Florida when they got to Florida. "How does Denny's sound for dinner?" She pointed with one hand to the restaurant coming up on their right. She pulled into the parking lot and turned off the car. "I'm hungry."

"Sounds good."

"I'll drive the rest of the way," Heather said when they returned to the car.

Joanne checked the door to the house before putting her key in the lock when they arrived. It didn't appear to have been tampered with. Hopefully, there would be no sign of squatters this time. She opened the door and went to help Heather retrieve suitcases and the few food supplies they'd stopped to purchase. "Everything looks the way we left it." She checked each room, satisfied no one had been squatting there. She plopped onto the couch and realized how tired she was from the drive.

"You rest for a while. I'll get the remaining things from the car." Heather carried in the suitcases and then joined her on the couch.

Joanne stood and stretched. "I'm going to search for bedding." She found sheets and blankets and made the beds before stopping in the kitchen to retrieve a beer for Heather and put water on to boil for tea. She settled next to Heather on the couch. "Let's relax."

Joanne turned on the television and sipped her tea. She felt safe with Heather sitting next to her, but would she sitting alone? She thought back to when she'd moved out of her parents' house. It was the summer she'd graduated from high school and planned her first semester of college. She considered all that had happened in her life since then and reached a place of calm. As if all of it was preparing her for this moment when she'd be on her own making her own decisions. Memories of her parents would always be there to comfort her, and Heather was in her life to help. This time in her life, this house left to her by her parents, and whatever the future held for her was all destiny. She looked forward to the future with all the new experiences that it would bring. "I think I'll be happy here." She turned to Heather and smiled.

"I'm glad. Just know that I'll only be a phone call away."

Joanne focused on the TV and began to drift into sleep within a few minutes.

"Hey, kiddo. It's been a long few days. I know I'm tired. How about we get some rest and go exploring tomorrow."

"I like that idea. We can pack a lunch and go sit by the water."

"Good idea."

Joanne put a few items in the empty dresser in what she now considered her bedroom and crawled into bed. She almost felt too tired to sleep, but she awoke the next morning and couldn't remember falling asleep. She rose to the scent of cooking bacon and smiled at Heather standing at the stove. "Good morning. Something smells delicious." She retrieved plates and silverware and set the small dining room table. She filled two glasses with orange juice and sat to wait for Heather.

"Did you sleep well?" Heather asked.

"I did. How about you?"

"Yes. No problem. It's nice and quiet here. I think you'll be fine."

"I agree. Knowing Betty is across the street helps, too."

"Let's eat and head out to explore." Heather filled both their plates with eggs and bacon.

Joanne gazed over the water when they parked in a nearby lot. "This is peaceful."

"It is," Heather agreed.

"I think I'll like living here. I know I won't miss the snow and ice in the winter."

"Remember that you can visit any time." Heather squeezed her hand.

"I know that, and I hope you'll come to visit me, too." She watched the waves on the shore similar to Lake Superior's. It soothed her in the same way, which reinforced her decision to move here. She often sat by the water to contemplate a solution to a problem or just to relax and meditate. This would become her new home, and knowing Heather would still be available calmed any lingering reservations. "I feel safe here." She smiled and hugged Heather. "I'm going to make it my home."

"I'm glad you have that option, Jo. I think your parents made a good choice buying the house here. If you change your mind I'll always be available to help you." Heather hugged her.

"Thanks. That helps a lot. My boss gave me a referral so I can get a job at one of our branches here, and I'm glad Mom and Dad furnished this place. I don't have to worry about moving any furniture."

"I think you'll be comfortable here. Let me know if I can help with anything."

Joanne took one last look at the water and followed Heather back to the car.

CHAPTER EIGHT

Shanna finished the sketch she'd been working on for two days and sighed as her mind wandered to her upcoming date with Barb. They'd spent three evenings together dancing and getting to know each other, and Shanna agreed to go out with her on an official date. She wasn't sure what to expect, but she felt comfortable with Barb. She didn't believe she'd push her into anything she didn't want. She put away her pencils and paper and checked the time. They'd agreed to keep things casual and planned on a dinner at a local restaurant so she chose a nice pair of slacks and a blouse. Barb arrived within ten minutes.

"Nice house." Barb walked through the kitchen as she spoke.

"Thanks. I just finished repainting it. Would you like a tour?"

"Sure." Barb followed her through the house. "Nice bedroom." She took Shanna's hand and pulled her close. "Shall we lie down awhile? I'd love to feel you next to me." She kissed her and tugged her toward the bed.

"I'm not comfortable with that, Barb. Maybe someday, but not yet." Shanna held her gaze and hoped Barb wouldn't push.

"Okay. But I hope we get to that point. I like you a lot, Shanna."

"I like you, too, Barb, but I need a little more time." Shanna took Barb's hand and squeezed gently.

"Let's go to dinner." Barb grinned and followed Shanna out the door.

❖

Shanna relaxed and sipped her coffee after they finished the meal. "This was nice."

"It was. I enjoyed the food and the company." Barb leaned back in her chair and smiled. "I hope we can do it again soon."

"I'd like to see you again, Barb, but I have to be honest with you. I'm not looking for a long-term relationship. I'm still recovering financially from my divorce and settling into living alone."

"No problem, Shanna. I'm not pushing for anything more than your company once in a while. I'm still healing from a nasty breakup, too. My ex left me for someone I considered a friend, so I have some trust issues."

"Sounds like we're quite a pair." Shanna raised her water glass. "A toast to healing energy."

"Healing energy." Barb raised her water glass and tapped it against Shanna's.

Shanna relaxed on her couch with a cup of tea after kissing Barb good-bye. She analyzed her feelings for Barb the best she could and decided she liked her a lot, and it felt nice to have a woman to date, but beginning a physical relationship concerned her. She'd been married to Paul for years with very little sexual interaction. She found Barb attractive and they probably would be good together, but something kept her from taking that step. She finished her tea and went to her studio to lose herself in her next project. She worked for an hour before putting her pencils away and heading to bed.

❖

The next morning, Shanna woke to bright sunlight streaming into the room. She stretched and enjoyed the feeling of freedom Sunday morning brought. Even though she worked from home she made it a point not to work on Sunday. No work today, no Paul to fix breakfast for, and no rush to get out of her pajamas. She made herself a cup of coffee and turned on the TV to the morning news. She propped her feet up on the coffee table as she sipped her coffee and considered what direction her life would take now. Barb was an unanticipated presence. As nice as it was to have a woman in her life to date, she wasn't sure her mother would agree. It probably wouldn't be an issue if she never came to visit, but Shanna looked forward to having her stay with her and they'd had the conversation regarding Shanna's sexual orientation before. Her mother would either accept her choices or she wouldn't. She finished her coffee and went to make breakfast.

Shanna finished eating, took a shower, and dressed before settling at her drafting table to sketch. She'd been working for an hour when her phone interrupted her. "Hi, Mom."

"Hello, dear. I just wanted to check on you. Are you all right alone there?"

"I am, Mom. I have my work and art as well as a few friends. Please don't worry. I'm fine."

"I'll leave you be, but my new neighbor has moved into her house. She'll be living there now and since she's your age, I thought it might be nice for you to meet her."

"Sure, Mom. I'll let you know when I can take a break from work and we can plan it."

Shanna put her drawing supplies away and turned the TV back on. She realized she wasn't paying any attention to whatever was on so she shut it off and picked up the novel she'd started reading a week ago. She set the book aside an hour later and turned on the television to the news channel. The weather report warned of a developing storm in the Gulf and she made a mental note to call her mother in the morning.

❖

"Did you see the weather report, Mom?" Shanna kept an eye on the TV the next morning while she spoke.

"I did, honey. It's not unusual for this time of year. It's probably nothing to worry about."

"I'm not sure. I think you better get ready to take shelter."

"I checked all my supplies yesterday. I'll be okay."

"All right. Don't forget you're always welcome to come here."

"I know, dear. I appreciate it."

Shanna made a mental note to keep an eye on the weather and went to work editing her next manual. She checked the news throughout the day, and her concern grew when she turned the weather on that evening. She picked up the phone to call her mom but hesitated when the weather reporter urged alertness but no warnings yet. She settled on her chair in her studio and began a new drawing. She sketched the scene in her head of the swaying palm trees and waves crashing on shore. She set her pencils aside and hoped the reality of the possible storm wasn't as severe as in her imagination. She checked the time and sighed with relief when the weather report showed the storm subsiding. She called her mom to make sure she heard the news.

❖

Shanna settled on her couch the next day and waited for Barb. They'd agreed to go to dinner and maybe watch a movie afterward. She looked forward to her company, but just as she considered calling Barb to cancel, her doorbell rang and she arrived.

"Hi there," Barb said as she held up a carry-out bag from Shanna's favorite restaurant.

"Hi, Barb." Shanna took the bag to the kitchen. "Thanks for bringing this. I'll admit I wasn't too excited about going out tonight. Okay if we just relax on the couch and eat?"

"Perfect. I just like spending time with you. We don't need to go anywhere." Barb kissed her lightly.

"I'm a little tired tonight." Shanna retrieved silverware and plates and settled on the couch next to Barb to eat. "Mind if I turn the news on?"

"Not at all." Barb propped her feet up on the coffee table and slid an arm around Shanna.

Shanna shifted slightly away from Barb's embrace as she took a bite of her food. She swallowed and sat up when the weather report came on. "This looks bad," she said between bites.

"They always make it look worse than it is. It'll probably rain a lot and move on."

"Yeah. Maybe, but they've been watching this storm for days. It could turn into a serious hurricane."

"We're safe here." Barb squeezed her hand.

"I'm not worried about us. I told you my mother lives in Fort Meyers. She's vulnerable."

"She'll be okay." Barb pulled her into her arms. "Why don't you let me distract you."

"I'm sorry, Barb, but I'm not interested in a physical relationship yet. Can we just relax together and watch TV?"

"Maybe I should leave you alone to obsess. I'll give you a call tomorrow. We can meet at the club Friday." Barb squeezed her hand, got up, and left.

Shanna sat stunned for a minute. She hadn't expected Barb to be upset by her refusal to get intimate, but maybe it was for the best that she left. She settled back on her couch to keep an eye on the weather. She was startled when her phone rang. "Hi, Mom. I was just thinking about you while I watched the weather."

"Hello, dear. I'm a little nervous about this new storm brewing, so I wanted to let you know I'm okay and I'll pay attention to the forecast."

"Good, Mom. Hopefully, it will fizzle out before it gets bad." Shanna disconnected the call and made herself a cup of tea before settling back on the couch. Her mind kept wandering to Barb and why she left. Perhaps all she wanted from her was sex. She'd never given Shanna that impression, but Shanna had been out of the dating scene for so many years she didn't trust herself to know the signals. She finished her tea and shut off the TV before going to bed.

CHAPTER NINE

Joanne pulled into her carport and shut off her car. She let out a breath and allowed herself to feel the pride that she'd driven Heather to the airport and made it home without getting lost. Her new GPS Heather had given her helped a lot and she planned to use it often until she got used to the area. She waved to Betty across the street and waited for her to come up her driveway. "Hi, Betty."

"Hi, Joanne. Have you heard the weather report lately?"

"No. I was visiting with Heather, and I just dropped her off at the airport. Why?"

"There's a storm forming in the Gulf of Mexico and it bears watching for us. It may fizzle out, but I think we should pay attention to the weather reports."

Joanne stared at her for a second and took a deep breath. She'd known Florida had hurricanes, but they were rare. She hoped. "Do we need to take shelter?"

"No. I don't mean to scare you, but let's go inside and watch the television."

Joanne opened her door and let Betty go in ahead of her. She turned on the TV and went to make them a cup of tea. "Have you lived through a hurricane before?" she asked.

"Yes. My husband and I experienced one the first year we moved here. It wasn't a huge one, but I was ready to turn around and move back to Illinois. We've had a few more over the years and lived through them, so I guess this one will come and go also." Betty sipped her tea and watched the weathercaster show the projected path of the coming storm.

"It doesn't look too bad," Joanne said.

"I hope it isn't," Betty whispered.

Joanne thought about all the tornado warnings they'd had and this didn't seem any worse. "I have homemade chicken noodle soup for dinner. Would you like to stay and join me?"

"Thank you. I'd love to." Betty took her empty cup to the kitchen. "Let me know if I can do anything."

"The water in the kettle is hot. You can pour us each another cup of tea."

Joanne spooned soup into bowls and Betty set full cups of tea on the table. She realized how comfortable she felt having Betty in her home and staying for a meal. Betty was her first friend in her new life, and she liked the feeling.

"I want you to know that we have someplace to go if we need to evacuate. My daughter has a house in South Carolina," Betty said between spoons of soup.

"I remember you mentioned that. I hope we don't need to go anywhere. I just moved here!"

"I hope so, too, Joanne." Betty sat across from her at the table. "You have a nice home here." Betty looked around the room.

"It is nice. I'm grateful for my parents' decision to buy it."

"So, are you here permanently now?"

"I am. I start work at the bank next week."

"Good. I'm planning a get-together for our neighborhood watch group on Saturday. I hope you can make it."

"I'll plan on it. Thanks." Joanne smiled, happy to feel like part of an important group.

After Betty left, she turned on her TV to pay attention to the weather. She put away the leftovers and loaded her dishwasher before settling on her couch with a cup of tea. Her thoughts strayed to the unpacked suitcase in the extra bedroom. She smiled at the knowledge she had an extra bedroom. Maybe she'd make it into an office. Or a game room. What kind of games she didn't know. Probably making it a guest room would be best. Heather said she'd visit. Maybe her friend from work would like to come to Florida for a few days.

Paula was a couple of years older than her, but they'd worked together for three years and gotten along well. Joanne was grateful when she asked to exchange phone numbers before she left. She'd called Stacy several times to let her know her plans to move, but never heard back from her. It saddened her that she couldn't even say good-bye, but Stacy had probably already moved on.

She relaxed on her couch and watched whatever was on television until she struggled to keep her eyes open. It had been a long day, and she was tired from the long drive. She changed into her pajamas and sat on the edge of her bed for a minute to gaze around her new bedroom. It was a nice room with olive-colored walls. She crawled under her covers and fell asleep within minutes.

❖

Joanne woke to sunshine. She turned on her side and soaked in the new view of her morning. She smiled at the feeling of freedom and security. She was in her own home in her own bed with the whole day ahead. She got out of bed and put on her robe before heading to the kitchen. She set up her coffee maker and turned on the TV to watch whatever was on in the morning in Florida. She set her coffee cup down and turned her full attention to the news and weather report. Betty's offer to go to her daughter's if necessary gave her a sense of security, but she hoped it wouldn't get bad enough for that. She went to the kitchen to search for breakfast food.

She'd just finished a bowl of oatmeal when there was a knock at her door. She checked the peephole, concerned the squatters were back. They wouldn't knock, would they? She was surprised to see her neighbor, and she opened the door. "Hi, Betty. Everything okay?"

"Hi, Joanne. Have you seen the weather this morning?"

"I did. It sounds like it'll be cloudy all day."

"I've lived here for several years and have gotten pretty good at recognizing dangerous looking storms. The one on its way is scary. I'm going to pack and be ready to leave if necessary. I hope you'll come with me."

Joanne sipped her coffee and considered Betty's offer. She certainly knew more about Florida weather than she did. "I appreciate the offer, Betty. Are you sure it'll be bad enough to leave?"

"I do, but we'll wait for the weather report later today. I'd be willing to stay until an evacuation order is issued, but we'll be fighting a lot of traffic. I'd suggest you be packed and ready to leave before that."

"I'll fill my car with gas." Joanne thought about the nightmare it would be for hundreds of people trying to leave at the same time.

"We can take my car, Joanne. It only has a few thousand miles on it, and I know the way."

"Okay." Joanne hesitated. "You sure we'll need to leave? I just got here and am settling in."

"Just be ready Joanne. If we don't get an evacuation order, we'll stay." Betty squeezed her hand and left.

Joanne walked through her house in a daze. How could she decide what to take and what to leave? She watched the weather report, but there were no evacuation orders. She tried to relax on her couch, but when Betty's warning kept invading her thoughts, she went to her bedroom to pack. She sat on the side of her bed and sighed. Only a few days ago she was packing to move here. She felt safe here. This was her home now and she didn't want to leave. She finished packing and realized she had no idea what South Carolina was like. She added an extra suitcase and went to talk to Betty.

"Hi there." Betty met her at the door. "Are you packed and ready to leave?"

"I think so, but I'm not sure what to take. Is it hot in South Carolina?"

"It is, but not quite as hot as Florida. You'll be fine."

"Okay. Then I guess I'm ready to leave. Are you sure we need to?"

Betty pulled her into a hug. "It'll be okay."

"I hope so." For the first time, Joanne became afraid, but took comfort in knowing Betty had a safe place for them to go. She went home to wait for evacuation orders she hoped never came. She walked through her new home hoping it would still be there if they had to leave. She made herself a cup of tea and settled on the couch to call Heather.

Heather answered on the first ring. "Hi, Joanne. Everything okay?"

"Yeah. Everything's fine. My neighbor thinks we may have to evacuate because of a hurricane. I'm a little nervous."

"I saw the storm on the weather channel. I think they expect it to lessen in severity overnight. I'm glad you have her to keep an eye on things."

"Yeah. Me, too, but I just moved here and I'm getting settled in. I don't want to leave it."

"It'll be okay, Jo. Better to be safe than sorry. If the Weather Service says go, you go!"

"I will. At least Betty has a place we can stay in South Carolina."

"Good. Let me know if you do evacuate. I'd like to know you're safe."

"Thanks, Heather. I will." Joanne went to her bedroom to review what she'd packed. Satisfied that she'd be set for a few days, she went back to her couch to keep an eye on the news.

CHAPTER TEN

S hanna watched the end of the evening news and paid close
attention to the weather report. The track of the hurricane
worried her, but there was no warning yet from the National
Weather Service. She knew her mother would keep an eye on it,
but she wrote herself a note to check on her again. She considered
skipping the trip to the lesbian club, but she'd told Barb she'd meet
her there so she changed and headed out the door. The room was
packed when Shanna arrived so she wound her way through the
dancers and women standing with drinks watching to a small table
along the side wall.

Barb arrived a few minutes later and joined her at the table.
"Hey. I wasn't sure you'd make it, but I'm glad you did." She took
Shanna's hand in hers.

"I needed to get away from the house for a while." Shanna
realized how true her statement was. At least when Paul was
around, she had some company. Living alone was peaceful, but
even with her work and sketching, she was feeling a little stir-
crazy. "Let's dance." She took Barb's hand and led her to the dance
floor. Shanna relaxed at the table after their dance and sipped a
beer. To Shanna's relief, Barb danced with several other women
throughout the evening. She liked Barb and hoped they could be
friends, but she wasn't interested in the "with benefits" part. She
lifted her bottle in a toast when Barb gave her a little wave.

Her thoughts strayed to her mother and the threatening storm. Her parents had lived in Florida for years and she knew her mom could take care of herself, but it never failed to worry her when dangerous weather loomed. She turned her attention to the dancers, sipped her second beer, and enjoyed the freedom to be herself.

"You doing okay?" Barb asked.

"I am. I'm enjoying relaxing with a bunch of lesbians having a good time."

"Feel like dancing?"

Shanna set her beer aside and stood to take Barb's hand. "I do."

She returned to her table breathless after dancing with several different women and couldn't remember when she'd had such a good time. "Thanks, Barb. I've had a fun evening." She stood and hugged her good-bye before leaving.

❖

She called her mother as soon as she got home.

"Hello, dear. Are you still worried about me?"

"I am, Mom. It looks like a dangerous hurricane on the way."

"I'm paying attention, honey. There'll be an evacuation order if it's necessary. Don't worry."

"Maybe you should just come here now. That way you'd be safe." Shanna began a mental shopping list.

"I promise I'll come as soon as it's deemed dangerous to stay. Okay?"

"Okay, Mom. Love you."

"Love you too, dear."

Shanna disconnected the call and wrote a note to shop for groceries in the morning. She turned on her TV and checked the weather channel every few minutes while she put clean sheets on her mother's bed and the bed in the guest room. She'd be ready if her mom and her friend needed a safe place to stay.

❖

Shanna's phone rang as she pulled into her driveway the next day. She grabbed a bag of groceries and took it into the house. "Hi, Mom. Are you leaving now?"

"We are. I just closed up my house and am helping Joanne load her things into my car. I guess you were right to be cautious. This storm looks like a big one. We'll be leaving in a few minutes, so I guess we'll probably get there after dark."

"Be careful. I just heard the traffic isn't too bad yet. Do you remember the shortcut I gave you from the last time?"

"I do and my GPS unit is set. See you soon, honey."

Shanna disconnected the call and began to put away her groceries as she wondered about her mother's friend. She jumped when her phone rang again. "Hi, Barb. What's up?"

"Hi, Shanna. A few of us are getting together at the club tonight. Would you like to join us?"

"Not tonight, Barb, but thanks for asking me. I'm preparing for my mom and her friend to get here from Florida."

"Are they just visiting?"

"The National Weather Service just issued a hurricane warning and evacuation orders for their area, so I'm getting ready for them."

"Geez. That's scary."

"I know. They won't get here until late, and I want to be here when they do."

"Okay. We'll get together another time."

Shanna began to answer and realized Barb had already hung up. She set up her coffee maker and put a kettle of water on the stove for tea before mixing the ingredients for bran muffins. The least she could do was have something for her guests to eat and drink after the long drive. Knowing her mother, she would only stop for restroom breaks. She settled on her couch to watch TV and follow the hurricane reports. "This looks bad," she said into the empty room. She checked the time and realized it was going to be a long night.

❖

She was startled awake by the sound of knocking, and she rushed to the door chastising herself for not leaving it unlocked. "Sorry, Mom. I didn't mean to lock you out," she said as she pulled the door open and faced a very attractive woman.

Her chocolate eyes sparkled as she smiled a tired smile. "Hello. I'm Joanne. May I come in?" She held up a suitcase in each hand.

"Of course. Come in, please." Shanna reached to take the suitcases and put them next to the door. She returned intending to help her mom with her luggage but found Joanne carrying them in and her mother following her.

"We made it, honey." Her mom looked exhausted.

"Come in and relax. I have tea or coffee with bran muffins." She realized she hadn't introduced herself to Joanne. "I'm Shanna. It's good to meet you, Joanne. Mom told me about you."

"She told me about you, too. I'm glad to meet you and I want to thank you for letting me come with your mom. I'll admit this is pretty scary for me."

"Mom told me you moved from Michigan."

"I did, and we have tornados there, but this hurricane terrifies me."

"You and Mom relax and unwind. I have your rooms ready whenever you want to go to bed. If you need anything, please ask." Shanna filled three cups with tea and carried them with three muffins on a tray to the couch. "I thought you might like to unwind after the long ride, but please don't feel like you have to stay up for me."

"This is perfect, honey." Her mother sipped her tea and took a bite of a muffin. "Once we got the word to evacuate, we packed, got in the car, and didn't stop except for gas until we got here."

"I'm glad you were with my mom, Joanne. That is a very long drive."

"It sure is! Your mom told me it was, but she made it sound like she'd done it often and not to worry. I'm glad I could be there to help her drive." Joanne drank her tea and took a bite of muffin. She swallowed and broke down in tears. "It was awful. So loud. I couldn't tell which way the wind was blowing from because it seemed to be coming from all directions. We stopped for gas, and I could barely stand to fill the tank because the force of the wind was so strong." She covered her face with her hands and continued to cry.

"It's okay now. You're both safe." Shanna wanted to wrap her arms around Joanne and comfort her. She settled for resting her fingers on her back and lightly rubbing it. "We'll relax for a few days and if you want to, we can watch the weather channel."

"I gave my friend Louise your phone number. She may call to check on us and we can find out if anyone is left on our street."

"Good idea, Mom. It'll be good to hear from your friend." Shanna hoped Louise hadn't been hurt in the storm.

"I'm exhausted. Thank you for the tea and muffin, honey, but I'm ready to fall into bed." Her mom stood and hugged her.

"Your room is the pale yellow one, Mom." Shanna helped her carry her suitcases into the room and turned down the covers for her. "I hope you sleep well and get some rest." She kissed her cheek before leaving her.

"I think I'll follow her lead. It just hit me how fearful this experience has made me. Thank you, again for letting me come along with your mom."

"No problem, Joanne." Shanna rose to lead her to her room. "The bathroom is across the hall and let me know if you need anything."

Shanna returned to the living room to watch the news and finish her tea. She hadn't asked her mother about her new neighbor when she'd told her about her and she certainly didn't say anything about how lovely she was. She put away the muffins and cleaned up the kitchen before going to bed. She was relieved to have her mom with her safe from the hurricane, but wondered how safe she was from the appeal of her young friend.

CHAPTER ELEVEN

Joanne woke to quiet in the dim light of early morning. Her first memory was the fear and frantic packing to escape the coming dangerous storm. She calmed as she snuggled under the warm comforter and crisp cotton sheets. She was safe and Betty was safe. Her very good-looking daughter had welcomed them with open arms. Her beautiful blue eyes had held compassion and welcome. She sighed and stretched before climbing out of bed and wrapping herself in her robe. She'd taken the time to open her suitcases to find essentials before sleep overtook her the night before. The very long drive wasn't as long as the one she'd taken to move from Michigan to Florida, but it was the most stressful she'd ever encountered. She'd moved to start a new life, and last night she'd run for her life. She was safe now. Her house and her new life in Florida was a memory overshadowed by the terror of a life-threatening storm. She'd lived through it and now she felt as if she were on the brink of an adventure. She pulled on her jeans and a sweatshirt before heading to the kitchen. Shanna stood at the stove cooking, and Joanne's mouth watered at the scent of bacon. "Something smells yummy!"

"I hope you like bacon and eggs because I just realized the only other breakfast food I have is oatmeal." Shanna smiled.

"It sounds wonderful. My breakfast usually comes out of a Cream of Wheat box, but I do like oatmeal." Joanne pointed to the coffee maker. "All right if I make coffee?"

"Please do. It's in the cupboard above." Shanna pointed with her chin. "I also have coffee pods for the Keurig."

She sat at the dining room table and sipped her coffee while she waited for Shanna. "Betty…your mom, isn't up yet?"

"Nope. She was completely worn out last night. I'll let her sleep as long as she likes."

"Thank you, again for letting me tag along."

"Joanne. I appreciate that my mom didn't have to make that long drive alone. I know that she would have tried, so thank you for going with her."

"Yeah. She was all packed and ready to leave when she pulled into my carport and demanded I evacuate with her. She might've saved my life." Joanne took a bite of eggs and bacon and moaned in delight. "This is fabulous. Thank you for making it."

"You're welcome. It's an easy breakfast to make."

"Cream of Wheat, remember?" Joanne grinned. "Betty said you lived here with your husband. Is he at work?"

"He and I are divorced now. He took a job in California, so I'm not sure if or when he'll be back."

"I'm sorry to hear that."

"What about you? Ever married or have a boyfriend? Girlfriend?"

"Huh. I thought I did, but it turned out she had more interest in herself than me. I'm single and probably will stay that way."

"Relationships can be difficult." Shanna shrugged.

"So, why did you think I might have a girlfriend?"

"I just get a lesbian vibe from you."

"I've never had a boyfriend."

"Good morning, you two." Betty shuffled into the kitchen as she spoke.

"Morning, Mom." Shanna stood and kissed her mom's cheek. "Did you sleep well?"

"Like a rock. Thank you, honey." She grabbed a cup and poured herself a cup of coffee. "Do you mind if I turn the TV on to watch the news?"

"Of course not. In fact, I'll join you." Shanna followed her mother to the living room and Joanne filled her coffee cup before joining them.

"It looks like we got away just in time." Betty shook her head as she spoke.

"Wow. There's a lot of damage. I hope our houses are still in one piece," Joanne said.

"Me, too." Betty leaned her head back and sighed.

"We can call one of your neighbors. They might give you an update," Shanna suggested.

"Yeah. Call Louise, Betty. Maybe things are okay." Joanne hoped for the best.

"I will later. I know she doesn't usually get up until ten."

"Mom. A hurricane just hit the area. She's probably up." Shanna handed her the phone.

Betty dialed her friend's number but was disconnected before the call went through. She tried twice more with the same result. "It's not going through. I hope she's okay."

"This not knowing is hard." Joanne stood and paced. "Maybe we could call the local police precinct."

"Let's finish breakfast first. Then we can get online and see what information we can find," Shanna said.

"Thank you, Shanna. For letting me stay with you and for being willing to get information for us." Joanne wanted to hug her but hesitated. Would it be inappropriate to hug her friend's daughter? She stayed in her seat on the couch.

"No problem, Joanne. I'm glad you and Mom are safe. I'd be worried sick if you two were still in Florida."

Joanne finished eating and gathered everyone's plate to take to the kitchen. She'd noticed the dishwasher earlier so she stacked them in it and found dishwasher soap in a cupboard. She started the washer and went back to the living room. "I hope you don't mind that I loaded the dishwasher and started it to wash."

"Not at all. Thank you," Shanna said. "You're pretty handy to have around."

Joanne blushed at the compliment.

"Let's check on the computer." Shanna retrieved her laptop to search for hurricane information. "It looks pretty bad. Not everything is destroyed though. Let's turn on the weather channel. It might have coverage of specific areas."

Joanne watched the coverage of crumpled buildings and overturned boats. The specific areas hit hardest seemed to be along the West Coast and the Keys. Fort Meyers was definitely in the path, but there was no coverage of her area. They'd have to go back to find out if there was any damage. The thought of making that drive back home held no appeal at the moment. She sipped her coffee and resigned herself to staying until Betty wanted to go home. She went to her assigned bedroom and called Heather.

"Hi, kiddo. How's Florida?"

"A mess right now. Have you seen the news?"

"I guess I better pay more attention. I've been in meetings for two days. What's going on?"

"A hurricane hit last night. I'm staying with a friend's daughter in South Carolina."

"Wow. But you're okay?"

"I am. It's safe here and Shanna is great. I'll go home as soon as it's safe to do so."

"Let me know if you need help. I'm done with the intense training I've been doing. In fact, I was thinking of planning a trip to visit you. Let me know when that'll work for you, okay?"

"I will for sure and you know you can bring your family with you. I'd love to see them again. It's been a long time. I suspect I'll have cleanup to do, but I'll let you know how it goes. Anyway, I just wanted to hear your voice. I miss you." Joanne held back tears. The fear, the long drive, and the anxiety over the future overwhelmed her. "Can I call you later?"

"Of course. Anytime, Joanne. I'm here for you."

"Thank you." She disconnected the call and took a deep breath before returning to the living room.

"Everything okay?" Shanna asked.

"Yeah." Joanne didn't want to get into the whole needing to talk to her therapist thing. "I wanted to check in with a friend. I knew she'd be worried." She refilled all their coffee cups and sat next to Shanna on the couch. "Anything new from Florida?"

"Cleanup crews are out and emergency services are searching for injured." Shanna took a drink of coffee before speaking again. "It'll take a long time to get everything back in order."

Joanne pushed down her rising panic. "It could easily have been me and Betty." She took a deep breath like Heather had taught her, and reminded herself they were safe.

"But it wasn't." Shanna rested her arm across her shoulder. "You're both safe and can stay as long as you need to." She squeezed her before dropping her arm.

"We'll be okay, Joanne," Betty said softly. "We'll get home as soon as we hear it's safe." She patted her knee.

Joanne smiled for what felt like the first time since the day before they left Florida. She would get back to her home in Florida and continue her life there. She relaxed and watched the coverage of the cleanup on TV. Her mind began to wander to what she'd left behind. Was the bank where she worked still there? She'd had the sense to grab her wallet and checkbook, but what good would it do her if the bank was gone? She picked up her phone and dialed the bank's number. There was no answer, but she got the voice mail and left a message. Did the bank have power if the voice mail worked? Her thoughts spun out of control, and just as she struggled not to panic, Betty reached and took her hand.

"It'll be okay. We'll get home and rebuild if we have to. Maybe we won't have to. Whatever happens, we'll get through it."

All Joanne could do was nod and hope that was true.

CHAPTER TWELVE

S hanna could see Joanne struggling but wasn't sure how to help her. She tried to imagine losing her home and relying on others for help. It would be scary at the least. She considered offering words of condolence, but they seemed hollow. "You know. You and Mom are pretty far inland. There's a possibility your area was spared from the worst of the storm."

"Maybe." Joanne smiled.

"I'll keep trying Louise's phone. I know she has a cell phone, so I hope we can get through. I'll try texting her, too," Betty said.

"She's probably dealing with her own living conditions, but hopefully she'll respond. Maybe the cell towers have been damaged," Joanne said.

"Let's watch a movie," Shanna offered. "We can catch up later watching the cleanup process."

"Good idea, honey," Betty said.

"I have a great comedy I watch when I feel overwhelmed with life." Shanna inserted the DVD into the player and settled on the couch next to Joanne. Their thighs touched, but she didn't move away. "I hope you like it. It never fails to distract me from my troubles." She started the movie with the remote as soon as her mother settled next to her. She enjoyed the sound of her mom and Joanne laughing next to her, and she hoped the movie was distracting enough to give them some peace. "I'll be right back." She went to the kitchen and returned with a bag of popcorn.

"What's a movie without popcorn?" Her mother and Joanne ate popcorn and relaxed and Shanna smiled. It felt good to be able to distract them from the disaster upending their lives.

She turned her thoughts to what to make for dinner, but decided she'd make tuna sandwiches for lunch and worry about dinner later.

"I'm going to try Louise again." Betty made the call and left a message when she got her voice mail. "I hope she calls me back." Betty frowned and Shanna rested her hand on her hers.

"I'm glad you got through, Mom. She's probably okay if her phone still works." Shanna was just talking to appease her mother's worry. There could be many reasons why Louise hadn't answered her phone. She hoped she'd get the message. "I'm making tuna sandwiches. Any objections?"

"Sounds good." Her mom and Joanne answered together.

"Can I help?" Joanne asked.

"You can keep me company," Shanna answered as she stood and went to the kitchen. "I have whole wheat and rye bread." She opened two cans of tuna and began mixing ingredients.

"I'll have whole wheat." Joanne searched cupboards to find plates and set them on the counter.

"Thanks for your help," Shanna said as she set sandwiches on the plates and arranged them on a tray to carry to the living room. "Hopefully, the news won't give us indigestion while we eat." She set the tray of sandwiches on the coffee table. "Anything new?" she asked her mother.

"Not really. This hurricane horror has devastated downtown, but the neighborhoods don't look too bad. At least the ones they've shown."

"I hope Louise can let you know how things are on your street."

"I hope so, too." Betty sighed. "I'm going to lie down for a while." She stood and turned toward her bedroom.

Shanna followed her. "Do you feel all right, Mom?" She rested her hand on her lower back.

"I'm fine, dear. I think the tension and the long drive have caught up to me. I'll just take a nap."

"Okay, Mom. Let me know if you need anything." Shanna made sure her mom was settled in bed before she returned to the couch.

"Is your mom okay?"

"I think so. This is the first time she's had to evacuate from her home. It's stressful, as you know."

"I do. Hopefully, we'll get good news from Louise, and I'll keep an eye on the news reports." Joanne picked up their coffee cups. "More coffee?"

"Yes please." Shanna relaxed on the couch grateful to have someone willing to help. "Thank you." She accepted the cup and smiled when her fingers grazed Joanne's.

Joanne settled next to her on the couch and sipped her coffee. "This might be getting old for you, but I need to thank you again for letting me stay here with you."

"You're right. It's getting old." Shanna grinned. "Would it help if I told you I like the company? I like your company? The house is too quiet with only me in it."

"Thank you. I like your company, too. I know you said you're divorced, but do you miss your husband?"

"No. I'm glad Mom's here, and I'm glad you came with her. I don't want Paul to return." Shanna took a drink of her coffee. "The news is back on. Shall we watch?"

"Absolutely." Joanne leaned toward the TV. "They're calling this hurricane a category two. I'll have to look that up. I know that there was a category five that hit a few years ago. That's the highest category I think, so I guess we can be grateful it wasn't that bad. The more severe storms seem to originate in the Atlantic."

Shanna patted her hand. "Yes. You and Mom may not have much damage." Shanna hoped her mother and Joanne would have homes to return to, but she liked having them there with her. She wanted more time to get to know the young woman seated next to her. "How old are you, Joanne?"

"I'll be thirty-four next month. Why?"

"Mom told me you recently moved to Florida from Michigan and now you're displaced and facing possible damage from a hurricane. That's a lot of stress yet you're sitting calmly drinking coffee here. I'm impressed with your maturity."

"How old are you?"

"Thirty-seven."

"Huh. That's not very old."

"No, it's not, but I'm not sure I could be as calm as you if I'd have gone through all you did."

Joanne shrugged. "I was born into the foster care system, so I learned to deal with chaos at a very young age. I lived with several different families until I was sixteen when my parents adopted me. My parents gave me security and taught me patience."

"They must be very special people."

"They were. They died in a car crash a few months ago. I found the deed to the Florida house in their papers and decided to move there."

"I'm so sorry, Joanne. Mom told me you moved here, but she never told me your parents were dead."

"It's okay. I think they'd be very happy to know I was here safe with you."

"I'm glad you're here and I know Mom is glad you're across the street from her."

"I was very happy to meet her. I have a friend, my therapist actually, who came to Florida with me. Your mom brought over a Bundt cake to share that day. It showed me what a nice lady she is."

"My mom's Bundt cake is legendary. She makes it for all the get-togethers in the neighborhood."

"I'll look forward to it. I'm planning to stay optimistic about our houses. The hurricane hasn't destroyed them."

"I'm going to check on Mom." Shanna quietly went into her mom's room and found her sound asleep. She checked the time and decided to let her sleep until dinner.

"Is she okay?" Joanne asked when Shanna returned.

"Yes. I'll let her sleep until dinner's ready. Do you like pork chops?"

"I do. There isn't much I don't like. Can I help with anything?"

"Set the table. We'll sit and eat like normal people and talk about anything except hurricanes."

"Sounds good to me." Joanne arranged three place settings on the table and filled glasses with water. "I'll check on Betty... your mom."

Shanna put the pork chops in the oven and followed Joanne. "Hey, Mom." She gently stroked her arm until she opened her eyes.

"Is it time to eat already?" Betty sat up.

"Almost. How do you feel?" Joanne asked.

"I feel better. I was exhausted."

"Good. We'll eat in about half an hour," Shanna said.

Shanna kissed her mother's cheek and followed Joanne to the living room. "I imagine you'd like to see what's happening."

"I would. Maybe they'll have expanded the area of coverage." Joanne sat on the couch and leaned toward the TV.

"I'm going to check the pork chops. Be right back." Shanna made sure the dinner wasn't burning and returned to watch the news with Joanne. "Anything new?" she asked.

"No. They're showing a lot of the damage in downtown Fort Meyers but nothing in the neighborhoods. We may not know what's going on until we get home."

Shanna watched Joanne's expression turn from intent to concerned, and she made a decision. "Let's eat. Then we'll make a plan."

Joanne was quiet while they ate and Shanna sensed her withdrawing. She reminded her of herself when she was in school and gotten a passing but low grade on an essay she'd worked hard on. Joanne was a grown woman who'd made a huge change in her life before having it turned upside down through no fault of her own. After they finished eating, Shanna put away leftovers and Joanne loaded the dishwasher. "Let's relax on the couch," Shanna said.

"Thank you for the dinner, honey," Betty said.

"Yes. It was great," Joanne added.

Shanna smiled at the compliment. "You're welcome. I have to say, you two are easy to please."

She watched the news report and began mental plans for a road trip to Florida.

CHAPTER THIRTEEN

The upcoming trip weighed heavily on Joanne's mind. It was difficult the first time when she and Betty fled the hurricane. This time they'd be heading home without knowing what to expect. She took a deep breath and slowly released it like Heather had taught her. She appreciated the calm that replaced the anxiety, and knowing Shanna would be going with them helped calm her nerves, too. She reviewed her bedroom to be sure she wasn't leaving anything behind and placed her folded clothes on the bed. She found Betty on the couch watching the news as they'd done every day since arriving. She paid attention but knew they were leaving no matter what and hoped their homes were still standing. She prepared herself to accept whatever they found but stopped and took a second look at Betty. "Are you feeling all right, Betty?" She looked pale and half asleep.

"I'm fine. I just think this whole stressful situation has caught up to me."

"You relax. I'll get you a cup of tea." Joanne made three cups of tea and took them to the living room. "My mother always said hot tea could fix anything."

Shanna joined them a few minutes later. "Thanks for the tea."

"You're welcome. I think your mom isn't feeling well." She felt Betty's forehead like her mother had done for her when she'd been sick. "I don't know for sure, but it feels like she might have a fever."

"How do you feel, Mom?" Shanna felt Betty's forehead.

"I'm just tired, honey. I'll be all right." Betty rested her head back after speaking and closed her eyes.

"Come on. You lie down in bed for a while." Shanna helped her mom to her bedroom.

"She felt like she has a fever to me. Do you think so?" Joanne asked when Shanna returned.

"Yes. I do. We'll let her rest and I gave her a couple of aspirin." Shanna settled next to Joanne on the couch and they both set their feet up on the coffee table. "It would probably be better if we wait a day or two to leave anyway. Give them more time to clean away the mess the storm made. They'll issue an all clear to return or something when it's safe for you to go back."

Joanne nodded and took a deep breath to calm her nerves. Her anxiety over the state of her house urged her to go home and assess the damage as soon as possible, but she didn't even have her car. She resigned herself to remaining patient. Besides, seated next to the beautiful Shanna on the couch was no hardship. "I'll make us some more tea." Joanne took their cups to the kitchen and returned with two full cups before going back and making one for Betty. She set it on her nightstand and settled back on the couch. "She seems to be sleeping peacefully."

"Good. This whole situation has been stressful for her. She's a strong sixty-two-year-old, but she had asthma as a child so even a slight cold knocks her out sometimes." Shanna reached for her cup and their thighs met. Joanne didn't shift away and hoped Shanna wouldn't either. Joanne considered Betty's age. "So she was twenty-five when she had you."

"Yes. I was a surprise baby but a welcomed one. Mom was twenty when her doctor told her that she and my dad probably couldn't have children. Five years later, she went to her gynecologist because she missed three periods and discovered she was pregnant."

Joanne never spent much time thinking about her birth mother, but Shanna's story reminded her of her own disability due to her disregard for the safety of her unborn child. "I'm glad she had you, and I'm glad I've met you." She smiled at Shanna's surprised look. "Thank you. I'm glad, too." She rested her hand on hers. My mom did right in bringing you with her."

Joanne turned her hand over and entwined her fingers in Shanna's. She smiled when Shanna didn't pull away.

"I should probably look in on my mom." Shanna squeezed her hand before releasing it and going to her mom's room.

❖

Joanne wanted to be ready if they were going to drive back to Florida so she pulled her suitcase out from under the bed and began sorting her clothes. The few clothes she'd worn while at Shanna's were still in the laundry basket Shanna had given her. She loaded them in the washer and wrote herself a note to check it later. She packed everything she could and left the suitcase on her bed. She went to the kitchen and poured a hot cup of chamomile tea for Betty. "I have hot tea for you, Betty." She set the cup on her nightstand.

"Thanks, Joanne." Shanna said as she placed a cold washcloth on Betty's forehead.

"How are you feeling, Betty?" Joanne asked.

"I'll be fine, dear. I'm just tired from all the stress, I think."

Joanne squeezed her hand. "Just rest. I'll let you know if there's any new news." She put her clothes into the dryer and went back to watching the news.

"She's asleep," Shanna stated when she returned to the couch. "We may have to postpone leaving a few days. I'd like her to be well enough to make the trip. It was about a ten-hour drive wasn't it?"

"Yes. It felt like a hundred, but it was about ten."

"We'll be all right. I'll make a list of food items to take along, but we need to be sure the authorities are allowing residents back."

Joanne's anxiety rose. She hadn't considered that they might not be allowed back yet, but maybe the roads were washed away.

She steadied her breathing and swallowed the threatening panic. "I never thought about that."

"It'll be okay." Shanna gently rubbed her back. "We'll take our time and be safe. I'll help you get home, Joanne."

"Thank you." Joanne's throat tightened and she swallowed hard.

"How about some more of that soothing tea? I'll make you a cup."

Joanne did deep breathing exercises while she waited for Shanna to return with the tea. By the time Shanna returned she'd convinced herself that everything would work out. She wasn't alone. "Thank you," she said when Shanna handed her a cup.

"I'm going to check on Mom." Shanna squeezed her shoulder before going to Betty's room.

Joanne sipped her tea and watched more of the coverage of the hurricane damage. She went to retrieve her clothes from the dryer, folded them, and packed them in her suitcase. She'd be ready as soon as they got the word they were allowed back.

"She's asleep," Shanna said as she settled back on the couch. "I'm a little worried that she won't be up to traveling very soon. She said she felt nauseous and wasn't too steady on her feet when she went to the bathroom."

"We'll keep an eye on her, but do you think we should call the doctor?" Joanne stood and began to pace.

"I think it's only a bug she picked up somewhere."

"But we aren't sick." Joanne stopped pacing and sat.

"People's immune system weakens as we age. Maybe she was run down because of the stress. If she gets worse, I'll call her doctor."

Joanne nodded and forced herself not to begin pacing again. She and Betty were safe and warm. There was nothing she could do about Florida but wait for word that it was safe to return. "Let me know what I can do to help."

"Thank you. I think you being here will help her know she's not alone with the tragedy. Joanne went to check on Betty and returned with her empty cup. "I'll refill it." She raised the cup before taking it to the kitchen. She set the full cup on the nightstand next to Betty's bed and felt her forehead before leaving. She sighed realizing they wouldn't be going back to Florida anytime soon. She returned to the couch and considered her options. "Your mom finished her tea so I gave her another cup."

"Thanks, Joanne. She needs to stay hydrated."

Shanna looked worried and Joanne wanted to help. "Shall we call a doctor?"

"I will if she gets worse. For now, we'll make sure she drinks fluids. I'll warm some chicken broth and see if she'll drink that, too." Shanna went to the kitchen.

Betty looked pale and vulnerable asleep on the double bed and Joanne wished she could do something to help her. She turned to leave the room when she heard a moan. "Betty?" she said softly.

"I need the bathroom." Betty began to sit up.

"I'll help you." Joanne wrapped her arm around Betty's waist and walked her to the bathroom. She waited outside the room until Betty called her name. "I'm here." She steadied Betty as she directed her back to bed.

"I'm sorry I got sick."

"Don't worry about it, Betty. Just rest and feel better. Florida isn't ready for us yet anyway." Joanne hoped she'd put Betty's mind at ease. She returned to the couch and updated Shanna.

"Thanks for your help. I know Mom is disappointed that she's the reason we haven't left yet, but I'm not sure the roads are clear enough anyway." She indicated the scene on TV of the ongoing cleanup process.

"Huh. Well, she needs time to gain her strength anyway." Joanne sipped her cold tea.

CHAPTER FOURTEEN

Shanna worried about her mother, but admitted to herself that she enjoyed having Joanne there. She was thoughtful and kind as well as being quite attractive. She hoped the hurricane cleanup went quickly, but she'd miss her when she went home. Her mom was getting stronger and Joanne had settled into a routine of care. She'd make tea or hot soup and make sure her mom finished it all. "You're pretty handy to have around," she told Joanne. "Thank you for all your help with Mom."

"No problem. She's my friend. Of course I'd help her, and I believe she'd do the same for me."

"Absolutely. I know she would," Shanna declared.

"I'm glad we heard from Louise yesterday. It sounds like we can probably head home at any time. Will you still be able to come with us?"

"I'll plan on it."

"I guess we'll play it by ear. Betty needs to be strong enough to travel."

"Yes, but we don't need her to drive. The two of us can handle it I think," Shanna said.

"Probably. Betty and I traded off driving and it worked fine." Joanne shivered at the memory. "It wasn't easy, though."

Shanna looked at her watch. "I'll check on Mom. Would you heat up the chicken soup please?" She stroked Joanne's hand.

"Of course. I'll bring her a cup when it's hot." Joanne squeezed Shanna's hand. "Why don't you sit a while?"

"I will after I check on her." She headed to Betty's bedroom but stopped halfway and turned to Joanne. "Thank you for all your help."

Joanne grinned. "You're welcome." She went to heat the soup.

"Are you feeling better, Mom?" Shanna asked as she tucked the covers in around her mother.

"A little, honey. I'm so sorry I'm delaying our trip. Has there been any new news?"

"Don't you worry about it, Mom. We'll plan the drive when you're feeling better. Just rest. Joanne is going to bring you some hot chicken soup."

"Thank you." Her mother drifted off after speaking.

"Do you think she's in danger of pneumonia?" Joanne asked when she returned.

"I'm worried about it." Shanna thought for a moment. "I'll call her doctor today. Maybe I can convince him to make a house call."

"That would be great. I'll give her the soup now."

Shanna hadn't been too worried until she heard her mother's cough. It sounded deep, and it scared her. She called and left a message for the doctor.

"I woke her to drink some soup," Joanne said as she showed Shanna the near empty bowl.

"Good." She gazed toward her mother's room. "Hopefully, she'll feel better soon."

"I never asked you what you do for work."

"I edit automotive manuals so I work from home. I'll help you both get home." Shanna rested her hand on her shoulder.

"I appreciate it, Shanna." Joanne hugged her.

Shanna slowly stepped out of her arms surprised by the spark of attraction. "Dr. Smith will be here soon. I'll let Mom know." She took a deep breath to try to expel the unexpected feelings holding Joanne generated. She made a cup of tea for her mom and took it to her room. "Hey, Mom. I brought more tea and Dr. Smith will be here later."

"Thank you, dear. I'm feeling better, but I really need the bathroom."

Shanna helped her mom to the bathroom and made sure she was settled back in bed before heading to the kitchen.

"How is she?" Joanne asked. "I'm heating more chicken noodle soup."

"She says she feels better, but I want to hear the doctor's opinion."

"I'd like that, too." Joanne poured some soup in a bowl. "Is she ready for more soup?"

"I think so. Leave it for her if she doesn't want it right away." Shanna left before she acted on her desire to feel Joanne in her arms again. She went to the living room to turn on the TV and watch the news. The coverage of the hurricane wasn't as extensive as it had been, but they showed downtown Fort Meyers. It looked bad. She made room on the couch when Joanne sat next to her.

"Anything new?" Joanne asked.

"Not yet. I'm hoping they'll cover the neighborhoods next."

"We may have to just head home and hope for the best." Joanne shrugged. "There's something else I'd like to talk to you about." Joanne looked serious.

"Sure. What's up?"

"I need to tell you that I like you a lot."

"I like you, too, Joanne."

"I guess I'm trying to say that I like you, and I'm very attracted to you."

"Oh." Shanna scrambled for a reply. She'd squelched her attraction to Joanne to keep things uncomplicated. She wasn't sure how to reply, or if she needed to.

"I don't want to make you uncomfortable. I thought Betty and I would be home by now and I'd never tell you how I felt. My therapist has told me several times not to keep my feelings bottled up, and I hope I haven't jeopardized our friendship."

"I'm glad you did. I like you a lot, Joanne, but right now all I can offer anyone is friendship." Shanna took Joanne's hand but refrained from kissing it. Worry over her mother and how or if she'd get her home to Florida kept her from admitting her attraction to Joanne. The doorbell interrupted their conversation. "Sounds like the doctor is here." She released Joanne's hand and went to let him in. "Thank you for coming, Dr. Smith."

"No problem, Shanna. Let's take a look at the patient." He followed her to Betty's room.

Shanna gently stroked her mother's cheek. "Dr. Smith is here, Mom."

"Hello, Betty. How are you feeling?" he asked.

"Tired," she whispered and closed her eyes.

He took her temperature, palpated her abdomen, and drew a vial of blood. "Has she been drinking water?"

"A little. Mostly hot chamomile tea and orange juice." Shanna made a mental note to give her water to drink.

"She seems a little dehydrated and probably has a flu bug."

"She hasn't been vomiting," Shanna said.

"Good. Keep an eye on her and make sure she drinks plenty of fluids. I'll give her a prescription for an antibiotic. Take her to the emergency room if she gets worse. I'll check back with you tomorrow."

Shanna thanked the doctor and locked the door after he left. She double-checked with her mom before going to the kitchen to check her supply of tea bags.

"How's she doing?" Joanne asked.

"Doctor thinks it's the flu. She needs rest and lots of fluids. I'm going to pick up a prescription for antibiotics. Will you be okay here with her?"

"Sure. I'll make her more tea."

"Thank you, Joanne. I'll be back as soon as I can." Against her better judgment, Shanna leaned and brushed her lips across Joanne's in a soft kiss.

❖

Shanna didn't have to wait long for the prescription to be filled when she arrived at the drug store, but almost wished she did. How would she explain the kiss to Joanne? Would it complicate their relationship? She was her mother's friend and she'd just given Joanne the "friends only" speech. The longer she obsessed about it, the worse she felt. She'd apologize and hope Joanne was okay with it.

She took a deep breath before opening the door when she got home. She went to the kitchen first to get a glass of water so her mother could take her pill. She let out a breath of relief when she didn't see Joanne. She relaxed on the couch to watch the news after giving her mom her pill and Joanne joined her.

"I'm glad you're back. Betty woke up and asked for you." She sipped a cup of tea. "I just checked on her, and she was asleep."

"Thank you." Shanna took a deep breath before continuing. "About that kiss. I apologize for taking you by surprise. I was out of line and it won't happen again."

"That's too bad. I wouldn't mind a repeat."

"You'll be going home to Florida as soon as Mom's well. I don't want to complicate your life."

"I'm not expecting you to marry me. I'd just like another kiss." Joanne grinned, lifted Shanna's chin gently, and kissed her. "That's all."

Shanna was glad she was sitting down. "Where'd you learn to kiss like that?" She steadied her breathing.

"You seem to bring out the best in me." Joanne sat back and continued. "I had a girlfriend in Michigan. Her name was Stacy, but it turned out my idea of a relationship wasn't the same as hers. She was the first woman I kissed. We did more than kiss, but that's not important. I learned how to kiss from her. You're the only other woman I've ever kissed." Joanne squirmed in her seat.

"I don't think that anyone teaches us how to kiss. I believe it's an automatic response. If we enjoy the person we're with, the kissing is good. If we just kiss for sake of kissing, it's sort of insincere."

"I guess. I told you I was attracted to you. Now that you kissed me, I seem to be obsessed with wanting more."

"I like you, Joanne. You'll be going home to Florida soon, and I'll be here working. I'm not sure it would be wise to get too close." Shanna sat back on the couch.

"Yeah. Maybe. Do you think matters of the heart can be controlled? Turned on and off like a switch?"

"No, I don't. Feelings of love are too authentic to be ignored or discounted. But, sometimes love finds us when the logistics are impossible."

"Impossible? It seems to me love is worth making possibilities. Making it a priority in life." Joanne took Shanna's hand. "I'm not expecting anything from you, Shanna, but I'd sure like another kiss." Joanne stood and went to check on Betty.

CHAPTER FIFTEEN

Betty looked better than she had for days and Joanne began to believe they'd get home after all. "Morning, Betty. You look like you're feeling better today."

"I am. Whatever Dr. Smith gave me is working. I feel a lot better. I think my fever is gone, too."

"We can confirm that." Joanne wiped the thermometer with alcohol and put it in Betty's mouth. "I'll be back shortly to check it." She took Betty's empty cup to the kitchen and refilled it with hot tea before returning to check her temperature. "Normal! You must feel better."

"I do, honey. I'm grateful for all your help. Is Shanna working?"

"Yes. Would you like more soup or I could make you a grilled cheese sandwich."

"More soup I think. My stomach is much better, but I don't want to overload it."

"Okay. I'll be right back." Joanne finished making soup and retuned to Betty. "Do you feel up to sitting on the couch? We can obsessively watch the news some more."

"I like that idea. I'll take a shower and dress first. We can surprise Shanna."

Joanne worried about her in the shower alone but wasn't sure how to offer help. "Do you think you'll need a hand getting in the shower?"

"I don't think so. It's a walk-in shower. I'll let you know when I'm in and when I get out. Okay?"

"Sounds good. Be careful." Joanne wasn't totally comfortable leaving Betty alone so she stayed close to her room so she could hear her if she called out. She sighed with relief when Betty stood at the foot of her bed fully dressed.

"That felt wonderful, dear. I feel like I'm back to the living." Betty went to the kitchen and stood looking around.

"You okay?" Joanne stepped behind her in case she felt dizzy.

"I'm fine. I'm just so happy to feel alive again." She picked up her cup and went to the living room. "Nothing new in Florida?"

"They're making progress on the cleanup. I'd like to try to head back as soon as you're feeling up to it."

"Give me a few days to get some strength back. I feel weak from lying in bed for over a week."

"Whenever you're ready." Joanne sat next to Betty on the couch and looked for any coverage of their neighborhood on TV. "It looks like they've stopped continuous hurricane coverage. I suppose it's old news now."

"Huh. For everyone except us. I guess we'll see what's what when we get home." Betty sighed.

"It'll be okay. Shanna offered to come with us by the way."

"Good. That'll make the drive easier." Betty rested her head back on the couch and closed her eyes.

Joanne made two cups of coffee and set one in front of Betty on the coffee table. She relaxed next to her and watched a talk show on TV.

"Did I fall asleep?" Betty sat up and rubbed her eyes.

"It's okay. You probably still need the rest." Joanne sipped her coffee. "I made you a cup." She pointed to Betty's cup on the table.

"Thanks." She took a sip and cradled the cup in her hands. "I'm glad you and Shanna are getting along."

"We are. I like her a lot."

"That's good. Very good." Betty sipped her coffee and smiled.

Joanne checked the time. "I'm making lunch soon. Are you sick of chicken noodle soup?"

"I sure am, but it's okay if that's all we have."

"I'll make us sandwiches to go with it." Joanne made lunch and made sure Betty ate before cleaning up. "Shall we look at a map so I can obsess over the drive home?"

"Sounds good. Let's review our route." She spread the map out on the coffee table and pointed out the road they'd taken to get to Shanna's. "It sure doesn't look as long on paper as it did when we were driving."

"It'll go faster this time because we're on the way home."

"I hope so. I'm looking forward to spending time in my own bed."

"I know, dear. I'm used to being with Shanna, so it isn't a hardship for me. I do look forward to being home though."

"We'll talk to Shanna about it later. She'll know when she'll be able to go with us, too. Would you like another cup of coffee or tea?"

"Thank you, honey. I'd love a cup of chamomile tea."

Joanne made herself and Betty cups of tea and carried them to the living room. "I'm getting used to this." She smiled and relaxed on the couch.

"I'm glad you're here, Joanne. I love my daughter, but it's nice having a friend here with me."

"I'm grateful you invited me along. I'm not sure what I would've done when the hurricane hit. Probably panicked and hid under my bed. I'd be in Oz now." She chuckled.

Betty squeezed her leg and went into her room before returning a few minutes later with a calendar. "Let's pick a tentative leave date."

"Okay with me, but we should probably check with Shanna."

"Yes, we will, but I'd like to have an idea of when we might leave." Betty studied the calendar for a minute and turned to Joanne. "Do you have plans to go home for Christmas?"

Joanne stared at her. "I've been so busy moving, settling in, and now fleeing from a hurricane, I forgot about Christmas. It's odd for me to be in warm weather in winter." She pushed aside her threatening depression along with memories of Christmases spent with her mom and dad. "This will be my first Christmas without my parents."

"I'm sorry. I didn't mean to bring up sad memories. I hope to be home for Christmas, but I suppose it'll depend on how much damage we have. Maybe we can plan to spend it together. Shanna usually comes to stay for a few days and I cook a ham." Betty sighed. "I'm feeling a little tired. I'm going to lie down for a while." Betty went to her room.

Joanne finished watching the news and turned off the TV. There wasn't anything new, and obsessing about the state of Florida after the hurricane wasn't doing her any good. She'd go home and see for herself as soon as possible. She retrieved one of her books and settled on the couch to read. She heard Shanna's voice half an hour later.

"Hi, Joanne. How's Mom?" Shanna went to the kitchen and grabbed a beer from the refrigerator. "Can I get you one?" she asked Joanne.

"No, thank you. I can't…don't…drink alcohol. I've got tea." She toasted with her cup. "Did you get all your work done?"

"I did. Thanks for keeping an eye on Mom for me."

"No problem. She's up and feeling better. We talked about when we'd leave for Florida. Will you still be able to go with us?"

"I'm looking forward to it. It'll be nice to get away."

"Let us know when you'll be available and we'll plan the date."

"I will. I'll go check on her."

"Good. We watched some TV earlier, and she ate some soup and a sandwich. She's lying down again now."

Joanne went back to reading until Shanna sat next to her. She enjoyed the heat radiating from her body and tried not to squirm at her sexual attraction. She needed to squelch that permanently. As far as she knew, Shanna could be looking for another man to marry. But what was that gentle kiss about? She pushed thoughts aside and concentrated on her book.

"Mom does seem a lot better. She told me you two started to plan the trip home," Shanna said softly and smiled.

"We did. We want to wait until you have the time off. Do you still want to go with us?"

"I do. I said I'd help drive and I will. I can take my work with me. As long as I have my laptop and an Internet connection, I'm good."

"Thanks. I hope you can stay with me a while when we get there," Joanne said.

"Sure. You're across the street from Mom, right?"

"Yes." Joanne smiled.

"I'm going to make a sandwich. Did you and Mom eat?"

"We did, but thank you." Joanne turned back to the TV for any news about being allowed back home. She wrote down the phone number for the information line and planned to call in the morning. She got up and went to the kitchen and found Shanna at the stove stirring something that smelled delicious. "What're you making?" She wrapped her arms around her from behind and pulled her against herself.

"Spaghetti sauce. Are you here to help?"

"I hope so." She hugged Shanna harder. "What can I do?" Joanne's thoughts raced from cradling Shanna's breasts and nuzzling her neck to stroking her belly and moving lower. She and Stacy had shared a pleasant physical relationship if not boring at times. Her feelings emerging for Shanna surpassed any she'd ever experienced. She released her hold on her and stepped back.

"You can set the table. I'd like to eat with a plate in front of me instead of on my lap."

"Okay." Joanne set the small kitchen table with three place settings and went to check on Betty. "Are you feeling up to eating at the kitchen table?" she asked when she found Betty seated in the chair next to her bed.

"I am." Betty followed her to the kitchen.

"I'm going to call my bank again tomorrow," Joanne said between bites. "I need to know if my checks are still good."

"I wouldn't be surprised if the banks and utilities in Florida have some sort of disaster policies. We don't even know if we have homes to go back to. I'm sure they'd be flexible." Betty patted Joanne's hand.

CHAPTER SIXTEEN

D inner will be ready in half an hour," Shanna called from the kitchen. She'd checked on her mother before beginning the meal preparation and her enthusiasm encouraged her. She'd been on antibiotics for four days and was almost her old self. She poured herself a glass of wine and settled on the couch to watch the news. The situation in Florida seemed to be settling down and she needed to plan their trip. She'd talk to her mom and Joanne about picking a day to leave.

"Something smells great," Joanne said as she sat next to Shanna.

"It'll be ready soon. Trust me, it's nothing exotic. Baked chicken with vegetables."

"Thank you for cooking. Thank you for everything, actually." Joanne rested her hand lightly on Shanna's arm.

"I'm glad I could help. And again, I'm glad my mom brought you with her." Shanna took Joanne's hand in hers and was pleased when she intertwined their fingers. She squeezed gently and suppressed her desire to kiss her. "I should check the chicken." She didn't move.

"Need any help?" Joanne asked but didn't let go of her hand.

Shanna wrestled with her feelings. She wanted to kiss Joanne and believed it wouldn't be unwelcomed. She pulled her hand away and went to the kitchen. She leaned on the counter and took a deep breath in an effort to squelch her bubbling desire for Joanne. She cleared her thoughts and began to straighten when she felt Joanne's arms slip around her from behind.

"Is this okay?" Joanne's breath warmed her neck and she shivered.

"Very okay." She turned in her embrace, gently cupped her face, and kissed her before she stepped back and turned to go to the living room.

"Wait," Joanne said softly. "I'll leave you alone. I just need to say one thing. That was the most awesome kiss I've ever experienced."

Shanna turned to face her and smiled. "Yeah. Me, too." She settled on the couch and turned on the TV to distract herself. She jumped at the sound of her doorbell. She opened the door and swallowed a gasp. "Paul?"

"Hi, Shanna. May I come in?"

"What are you doing here?' She spat out the words ready to close the door in his face.

"I took a few days off and wanted to see you."

"Well, I'm busy. Mom's here and just recovering from the flu. Sorry you came all this way for nothing. Good-bye." Shanna closed the door and locked it.

"Sorry about that."

"Was that your husband?"

"Ex-husband. Yes. I don't know what he expected, but he needs to go away."

"I hope we aren't keeping you from talking to him. I know what it's like to have unfinished business with someone." Joanne frowned.

"You're not. I have nothing to say to him that I haven't already said. I bet his girlfriend found out he wasn't who he presented himself to be."

"Ah. Well, I hope he leaves you alone, then."

Shanna took a deep breath and went to check on her mother. "You doing okay, Mom?"

"I'm fine, dear," Betty said from her bed. "I'm just still a little tired. Probably from the flu."

"I'll get you a cup of hot tea. You just rest."

"She okay?" Joanne asked when Shanna returned to the kitchen.

"I hope so. I'm getting her more hot tea. I'll call the doctor again if she doesn't bounce back soon."

"She seemed to be doing so well." Joanne looked worried.

"I think she'll be fine. She's just run down with the worry about the hurricane." Shanna hoped that was all there was to her mother's weakness.

"Yeah. I'm still a little worried, too. I'll try to call Louise again. Maybe she has some information about what it's like in Florida now. If things are clear enough, and you're willing to help me drive, Betty can just rest on the trip."

"That sounds good. We'll try Louise tomorrow again if you don't reach her." Shanna relaxed knowing they had a plan. How she'd explain Paul to Joanne was an unknown.

"Are you okay?" Joanne asked.

"Yeah. I'm just a little unnerved by Paul showing up. He told me he went to California. He must be back if he bothered to come here." Shanna shrugged.

"Maybe he missed you and regrets leaving."

"He knows I don't want him. He must've broken up with his girlfriend and hoped I take him back."

"I hope us being here isn't causing you problems," Joanne said.

"Not at all. Paul moved to California, and I have no idea why he came back."

"I'm going back to obsessively watching the news, but I'll check on Betty first if that's okay with you."

"Absolutely. Let me know what she says." Shanna sat in her recliner to watch TV.

Joanne returned from Betty's room and sat on the end of the couch. "I promise to leave you alone if you want to sit on the couch."

"No. I'm fine, Joanne. I don't want to make you uncomfortable. I'll admit you make me feel things, but not uncomfortable." Shanna grinned.

"I'll miss you." Joanne spoke so quietly Shanna almost didn't hear her.

"Yeah. I'll miss you, too." Shanna scrambled for more to say. "We could visit."

"Maybe so." Joanne looked conflicted. "I guess we need to get home before making plans."

"We'll figure it out. First, we have to get you and Mom home." Shanna went to check on her mom.

"Is she feeling better?" Joanne asked when Shanna returned.

"She is." Betty grinned and settled on the couch. "I'll be fine. How do things look?" She turned her attention to the television.

"I think they're making progress getting the roads cleared," Joanne said. "I wrote down the phone number they just showed for information. We can call to find out if our area is allowing residents back yet."

"That's good news." Shanna wanted her mother to be well and happy at home, but she'd gotten used to having Joanne around and knew she'd miss her a lot.

"Anybody ready for some leftover spaghetti?" Shanna asked from the kitchen.

"Yes," they both responded at once.

Shanna filled two plates with spaghetti and took them to Joanne and her mother. "I'm glad you're feeling better, Mom."

"Thanks for making this, Shanna," Joanne said.

"You're welcome." Shanna took several deep breaths. She didn't want to admit how much Paul's return upset her. She'd relaxed into a life without him and hoped never to see him again. She took a swallow of wine and poured the rest out of her glass. Too much wine would only make her sick. She went back to the living room.

"You okay?" Joanne asked.

"Yes."

"You sure?" Joanne stroked her arm. "I'm not sure I believe you."

"I'm okay. I was just thrown by Paul showing up today. I'll be okay."

Shanna shifted in her seat and tried to hide the tremble in her hands. "You are not okay." Joanne wrapped her arms around her and held her close until Shanna's trembling stopped. "Paul's gone. It sounded to me like you told him never to come back." Shanna didn't realize she was rocking in Joanne's arms.

Shanna sat up and settled herself with deep breathing. Paul was gone, Mom was getting better, and Joanne sat with her arm around her. They were safe. She wasn't alone. "Thank you, both for being here."

"Thank you for having us," her mother said.

"Yes. We'd be who knows where running from the hurricane." Joanne hugged her tighter.

Shanna smiled and gently squeezed her arm. "I'm making hot chocolate." Shanna went to the kitchen and returned with three cups. She settled back on the couch next to Joanne. "This is nice."

"It is. Thanks." Joanne slipped her arm around Shanna.

Shanna leaned into her embrace grateful for the heat of her body and her gentle touch. "I could get used to this," she whispered.

Joanne leaned into her and sighed. Shanna sipped her hot chocolate and decided she didn't want to move. "How are you feeling, Mom?" she asked.

"Much better, honey. This hot chocolate has hit the spot. Thank you for making it."

"You're welcome. I thought we needed something different." Shanna finished her hot chocolate and set her cup down. "I was afraid the hot chocolate would keep me awake, but I feel ready to fall asleep." She rested her head on Joanne's shoulder and closed her eyes. Shanna realized she'd fallen asleep and sat up quickly. "Sorry." Joanne stroked her cheek and spoke softly. "No problem. I like to feel you next to me." She hugged her closer.

"Are you two interested in some ice cream?" Shanna asked, trying to dispel her embarrassment.

"I am!" Betty said.

"Sure. I love ice cream." Joanne sat up.

Shanna went to the kitchen and took a deep breath to settle her intense reaction to being so close to Joanne. She returned with three bowls of strawberry ice cream and sat next to her mother.

"I'm going to miss this when I go home," Betty said. "Thank you for giving me a safe place to stay, honey."

"Mom. You're welcome here any time you want to come. Hurricane or not."

CHAPTER SEVENTEEN

Joanne shifted in her seat after Shanna left, leaving behind a cold spot where she'd been. She smiled at Betty who dozed next to her. The driving on the trip home would probably fall to her and Shanna. Betty could relax and snooze in the back seat. "Thanks for the ice cream."

"You're welcome. I consider ice cream a staple. I'm rarely without it." Shanna's smile warmed her in places she tried to ignore but found impossible.

"Ice cream has arrived," she said loud enough to wake Betty.

"Thank you, honey." Betty took a spoonful of ice cream as soon as she had the bowl. "Yum!"

Joanne thought back to the day they'd arrived and the welcome she'd felt. She hadn't known anything about Shanna except that she was Betty's married daughter. The longer they extended their stay, the closer she felt to her, and the more she liked it. She admitted to herself her growing feelings for Shanna and forced herself to ignore the fact that she might be straight and lived over five hundred miles away. The fact that her ex-husband wasn't completely out of the picture was something she couldn't ignore. She and Shanna worked well together, and relaxing on the couch with her felt like the most normal thing she'd ever done. She didn't even try to compare her feelings for Shanna to hers for Stacy. She sighed and turned her attention to Betty. "Is strawberry your favorite?"

"I like any kind of ice cream," Betty said after swallowing.

"Yeah. Me too." Joanne wondered why Shanna hadn't returned to the couch. "I'm not crazy about nuts in ice cream."

"Nuts, cherries, strawberries, it doesn't matter to me as long as it's ice cream." Betty set her empty bowl on the end table.

Joanne picked up their empty bowls and took them to the kitchen where she found Shanna at the sink. "Thanks for the ice cream. It was a great distraction."

"I have another one." Shanna turned and cupped Joanne's face in her hands and kissed her. The passionate kiss took Joanne's breath away, and she returned it enthusiastically.

Joanne found herself pressed against the counter, and she never wanted to move. She moaned and Shanna leaned into her molding their bodies together. She felt Shanna's breasts against hers and her nipples hardened. She wasn't sure she could breathe but didn't care as long as Shanna never stopped kissing her. She gave in to her need to feel more and pushed her hips forward as she gripped Shanna's ass and pulled her against her.

Joanne's lust-filled brain registered they were standing in the kitchen and Betty could walk in at any time. She gently pushed Shanna away, separating their bodies a few inches. "Your mom might come in looking for me." She took a shaky breath.

"Yes. Sorry. I didn't mean to attack you like that."

"Please, Shanna. Do not apologize for wanting to kiss me. I've been fighting that desire myself for days."

Shanna stepped away and turned toward the counter. "I'll be right out." She picked up the two bowls of ice cream that were starting to melt.

"I'll save you a seat." Joanne stroked her back before leaving the room.

"I thought you got lost in there," Betty said.

"I helped Shanna. She'll be here with more ice cream soon." Joanne sat in what now felt like her seat on the couch and waited for Shanna. She hoped she looked relaxed instead of how she felt. Like she wanted to throw herself on top of Shanna when she returned to the couch.

Shanna set three bowls of ice cream on the coffee table and sat as far as she could away from her. Joanne cringed at the withdrawal even though she understood it. She had no business kissing a possibly straight, in the middle of getting a divorce woman, who'd offered her home for safety. But Shanna kissed her first, didn't she? She picked up a bowl and spoon and concentrated on eating. Her attention quickly turned to the television. The coverage of the damages from the hurricane had been expanded to the neighborhoods. "Have you seen our street, Betty?"

"Not yet. I hope they show it soon."

Joanne stayed seated at the end of the couch being careful not to touch Shanna. She needed to let Shanna determine the nature of their relationship and ignore her desire for another kiss. Her body still tingled from the feel of her pressed against her, and she forced away the image of them together naked. She finished her ice cream and leaned back on the couch. "I suppose we need to think about packing." She mentally reviewed how much she'd already packed and relaxed. She could be ready whenever Betty wanted to leave.

"There's no rush," Betty said. "I'd hate to get there and find our homes unlivable."

"Don't worry, Mom. You can always come back here. Both of you." Shanna smiled.

"Thank you, dear, but I'd like to get home if possible." Betty sighed.

"I appreciate it, Shanna," Joanne said. "It helps to know I wouldn't be homeless." Joanne considered her options. She could always go back to Michigan and stay with Heather until she found an affordable apartment. She shook off the anxiety the thought brought and concentrated on the news. "Look, Betty! Isn't that the Johnsons' house?" She pointed to one of the homes featured on the news.

"I think it is. They're only a block away from us. Maybe we'll be okay."

Joanne watched intently and hoped for good news about her house. "It looks like the state is doing a good job with the cleanup."

"It sure looks promising," Shanna said.

Joanne watched as the news report covered a few areas but never their street.

"Yeah. Maybe we should pick a date and just go."

"That would give us a goal." Shanna looked thoughtful. "Let's try to call your local police department. They should have some knowledge of how things are."

"I'll check my neighborhood phone directory." Betty went to her room and returned with a small booklet. "The local police number is right here." She handed the book to Shanna. "I forgot to put my phone on the charger."

Shanna called the number on Betty's booklet and left a message when she got their voice mail. "I bet they're swamped with calls."

"Maybe we will just have to go back and take our chances." Joanne held back tears. She'd hoped for good news.

"Okay. That's what we'll do." Betty stood and went to her bedroom. "I'm going to pack."

"When Mom calms down, we'll plan the trip. Are you okay with that?" Shanna asked Joanne.

"Sure. I think Betty is feeling better, but maybe a little displaced."

"You're perceptive. She's a homebody. She loves me to visit her but doesn't like being away from home for long."

Joanne went to her room and sorted through her clothes. She sat on the bed to evaluate her feelings. She wanted to go back to check on her house and finally settle there, but her shared kiss with Shanna felt like unfinished business. She needed to know if it had affected Shanna as much as it had her. And what did it mean if it did. She couldn't see a future with her if her husband came back. Would she choose to go back to him? She'd said she didn't want him back, but what could she offer her besides a life in Florida with someone so flawed? No. She deserved to be with a lover with more to offer. That fabulous kiss they shared would have to last her forever. She checked the closet and made sure she wasn't leaving anything before closing her suitcase and putting it on the floor.

"How does baked pork chops sound for dinner?" Shanna asked.

"Sounds great to me." Joanne appreciated Shanna's attempt to make things feel normal. Like she wasn't prepared to leave and perhaps never see her again. She went to Betty's room to check on her. "Need any help?"

"I'm all set, honey. Thank you for asking. We're not leaving yet."

"I know. Shanna's making baked pork chops. We don't want to miss that."

"Are you okay with the decision to leave soon?" Betty asked.

"I am. I'd like to get back and check on my house, but it's been great staying here with Shanna."

"Yes. I can see that you two have gotten close. She'll come to Florida to visit. Especially now that Paul is gone."

"I hope so. I'd like that."

"I'm sorry if I'm pushing you, but I'm worried about my house. I'm anxious to get back."

"No problem, Betty. We'll head home as soon as Shanna has time to help us drive."

"Okay, but I feel pretty good now. I think we could make it without her."

"We're not leaving right away, so let's decide in a few days." Joanne hugged Betty and followed her to the kitchen.

"Can I help with anything?" Joanne asked.

"Everything's done except the salad. You can help me put that together."

Joanne retrieved the salad fixings from the refrigerator and combined them in a large bowl. She set the bowl on the table. "Which salad dressings do you like?" She held the refrigerator door open waiting.

"All of them," Betty said from the table.

Joanne smiled and set all four dressing selections in the middle of the table before sitting next to Betty. "Thanks for making this." Joanne smiled at Shanna.

"No problem. I'm glad for the company. I got used to eating alone. I never knew when or if Paul would come home."

Joanne didn't ask the question on her mind. Why would someone as beautiful and smart stay with someone who treated her like that? Shanna deserved better.

CHAPTER EIGHTEEN

Is everything okay, honey?" Betty asked. "You're awfully quiet."

"Everything is fine, Mom. I'm just a little sad that you're leaving. I've gotten used to the company." Shanna poked at her salad.

Betty swallowed before speaking. "We're not leaving yet."

"I know. But it probably won't be long now. Florida seems to be bouncing back quickly."

"We'll check with the police again before we leave. If they tell us to wait a while, we will." Joanne rested her hand on Shanna's.

"I guess I've gotten used to having you two here. I'm sorry. I know you have lives in Florida."

"And you are welcome anytime to visit and stay as long as you like." Joanne squeezed her hand before letting go.

"And I hope you will come back to visit again under better circumstances."

"Yes. I hope never to have to worry about a hurricane again," Joanne said and stabbed a piece of meat.

"I hope you don't either," Shanna replied.

"I'm afraid it's almost a given if you live long enough in Florida," Betty said.

"Well, it probably won't happen again for a while."

"Probably not." Betty smiled.

Shanna began to load the dishwasher when Joanne gently took her hand and spoke. "Let me do that. You cooked. Betty might like a cup of tea."

"Thank you." Shanna made tea while Joanne finished the cleanup. She liked watching Joanne at the sink rinsing dishes then putting them into the dishwasher like she'd done it her whole life. She could get used to having her around. She wasn't sure what that meant, but she pushed aside anymore thoughts of it for now. "Thanks again for your help."

Joanne turned to face her and leaned back against the kitchen counter. "It doesn't sound like Paul helped much."

Shanna sat at the table with a cup of tea. "For the last couple of years, Paul was rarely home. He told me he was working late and was trying to make partner in his law firm. I'll probably never know if it was true, but I don't care anymore. I'm glad he's out of my life."

"Why do you think he came back?"

"I don't know and I don't care." Shanna sipped her tea.

"Is your mom lying down?" Joanne asked.

"Yes. I took her a cup of tea."

"I hope she'll be up for the trip home. She still seems a little weak." Joanne looked worried.

"She'll be okay. You and I can do the driving." Shanna started at the knock at the door.

"Hey. Sorry to just drop in unannounced, but I missed you." Barb stepped into the room, cupped her chin, and kissed her.

Shanna stood stunned for a moment. "Barb. What are you doing here?"

"I haven't seen you at the club for a while. I've missed you." She leaned to kiss her again, but Shanna stepped back.

"My mom is here from Florida, and she's just recovering from the flu. I'll let you know when I'm available." She opened the door and waited for Barb to leave.

"Okay. I'll be at the club next Saturday." She walked out the door.

"Sorry about all that," Shanna said and wondered what Joanne thought of her now.

"No problem. We're here interrupting your life. I hope you're not staying home just because we're here."

"I'm not. Honestly."

"Okay. But please let me know if I'm in your way. For anything." Joanne looked upset.

"I will, but it's not an issue." Shanna rested her hand on her shoulder. She smiled and went to check on her mom.

"You doing okay, Mom?"

"I am, honey. I was packing and decided I needed a nap. I seem to run out of energy quickly now."

"That's okay. There's no rush for anything. Rest when you need to, and things will get done when they get done." Shanna kissed her cheek and went back to the living room. She tried to push away her worry about Barb showing up. It bothered her that she felt she could show up and kiss her uninvited. She did miss going dancing at the club though. She needed to talk to Joanne. It wasn't fair to kiss her and then have Barb show up and kiss her, too. Especially when it was only Joanne she wanted to kiss. She sighed knowing it was a bad idea. Joanne would be leaving for Florida soon and she would miss her. She watched a little bit of the hurricane news and switched to a game show. She enjoyed the diversion from the constant news.

"Mind if I join you?" Joanne asked.

"Not at all. I'm tired of the constant news though. I thought watching someone spinning a wheel was a good diversion."

"It is. Maybe Betty would like it, too."

"She's resting again. I'm a little worried about her recovery. She seemed to be getting over this bug, but this evening she's wiped out."

"Is she done with the antibiotics?" Joanne sat next to her with her leg pressed against hers.

"Yes. If she gets worse I'll call the doctor." She automatically leaned into Joanne's embrace when she rested her arm around her shoulders.

"Who was that woman who came over earlier and kissed you?" Joanne said softly.

Shanna considered not telling her, but she had nothing to hide and she could understand Joanne's curiosity. "She's someone I met at a club I went to a couple of times." She hoped Joanne would accept that as enough.

"She seems to like you a lot."

"We went on a date once. We went to dinner. That's it."

"You were married to Paul, but you're divorced now. What does that mean?"

"I don't know, but I know that I'm attracted to you."

Joanne squeezed her hand. "I have growing feelings for you. I haven't sorted them out yet, but it's more than just liking you."

"It's okay. We'll figure it out." Shanna leaned into Joanne and kissed her. "Would you go on a date with me?"

"Sure. Where're we going?"

"Let's go dancing." Shanna grinned and tamped down her anticipation of holding Joanne in her arms.

"What about Betty?"

"I'll make sure she's okay for a couple of hours. We don't have to stay late."

❖

Shanna relaxed when she didn't see Barb at the club. She took Joanne's hand and led her to the bar. "I'm having a glass of wine. What can I get you?"

"I'll have a Coke, please." Joanne followed her to a table.

"They play a nice mix of fast and slow music here." Shanna sipped her wine and held Joanne's hand as she spoke.

"I don't think I'm a very good dancer," Joanne said.

"Let's find out." Shanna took her hand and led her to the dance floor.

Shanna held Joanne close as they moved to the music. She hadn't known what to expect after Joanne's statement, but she turned out to be a good dancer. At least they were good together, and she liked it. "You're a good dancer, Joanne," she whispered in her ear.

"I think it's because I'm dancing with you. It feels good to hold you."

"I'm glad you agreed to come with me."

"It's fun. I've never been to a bar filled with lesbians before."

"There aren't many left I'm afraid, and women only show up here after seven o'clock."

"Thanks for bringing me." Joanne kissed her quickly.

"This is fun," Shanna said. "We're good together."

"We are," Joanne agreed.

"We should probably head home soon. I left a note for Mom, but she may worry." Shanna finished her wine and stood.

"Thanks again for taking me tonight. It was a fantastic evening."

"It was." Shanna took her hand very glad Barb hadn't shown up.

"I hadn't realized how anxious I was about getting home. This helped distract me." Joanne squeezed her hand and kissed her softly. "That helps, too." She grinned.

Shanna drove one-handed while holding Joanne's hand. "I'm glad you had fun."

"I did. I told you I had a girlfriend in Michigan, but we rarely went anywhere fun. Stacy was pretty much only interested in shopping or walking in the mall."

"Do you miss her?" Shanna wasn't sure she wanted to hear the answer.

"Not at all. I don't think I was too important to her. Her response to me when I left her a message about me moving to Florida was 'there are scorpions and alligators in Florida.' I don't think she'll ever come to visit."

"I'm sorry to hear that. You deserve better."

"Yeah, my friend Heather told me that, too."

"Heather?"

"She's been a friend of the family for years. She helped me move."

"I'm glad you have her. I hope to meet her one day."

"She likes to visit Florida, so we'll have to make it happen."

Shanna parked her car in the garage and turned in her seat to kiss Joanne.

"Maybe we should take this into the house. These car seats aren't too comfortable," Joanne said between kisses.

"Good idea." Shanna led the way into the house.

"Are you home?" Betty called from her room.

"We are, Mom. You feeling more rested?" Shanna went to check on her.

"I am, honey. Did you two have a good time?"

"We did. It was fun." Shanna hoped her mother would stay in her room. She wanted to finish what she and Joanne had started in the car.

CHAPTER NINETEEN

I'm glad you're feeling better, Betty. We can probably plan to leave any time now. I called our local police and they told me we're allowed home. Our area is deemed safe enough."

"That's good news! I can be ready whenever you want to go, Joanne."

Joanne went back to the kitchen where she'd seen Shanna. "It sounds like your mom is ready to leave anytime." She took Shanna's hand and kissed it. "I'd like to finish what we started in the car." Joanne hesitated. She'd never been the one to initiate intimate contact because Stacy liked to be in control. She hoped Shanna still wanted more kissing.

"I would, too." Shanna spoke softly. "I'm going to heat up the last of the leftover spaghetti for Mom first."

"I'll heat some up for us if you'd like. I'm hungry."

"Me, too. Please heat some for me." Shanna put her spoon down and kissed her.

Joanne leaned into the kiss and wrapped her arms around Shanna's waist. Shanna whispered in her ear. "Stay with me tonight?"

"I'd like that."

Shanna took her mother her meal and Joanne heated spaghetti for them. She had two plates full and sitting on the table when Shanna returned. "Mom's feeling much better. I think we can probably be ready to leave soon." Shanna finished eating and put the dishes into the dishwasher before taking Joanne's hand and leading her to her bedroom.

"Will your mom get up and look for you?" Joanne asked.

"No. She could barely keep her eyes open when I checked on her after she ate." Shanna closed her bedroom door and locked it before turning back to Joanne and kissing her.

Joanne leaned into the kiss and pulled Shanna against herself. She broke away from the kiss to catch her breath. "I've never felt this way before." She went back to kissing her and Shanna pulled them down on the bed.

"Let me know if you want to stop," Shanna said softly while she traced a path with her fingertips along Joanne's face, chin, and neck. She kissed her and continued exploring her body.

Joanne squirmed under Shanna's gentle touch. She'd been intimate with Stacy but never felt anything like she did being with Shanna. She pulled her against herself and shuddered as her orgasm rippled through her.

"You okay?" Shanna asked and kissed her lightly.

"Oh yeah. Very okay." She rolled on top of Shanna and began her own exploration. She forced herself to breathe as Shanna writhed beneath her touch. "I love touching you." She stroked Shanna's upper thigh and slowly moved toward her heat. She wanted to make Shanna feel as good as she'd felt. She began with a gentle stroke and increased the pressure when Shanna sat up and pushed her fingers against herself. Joanne went with her instincts and slowly slid her finger into Shanna's wetness. Shanna plopped onto her back and trembled as she orgasmed. Joanne wrapped her in her arms and kissed her. "I love touching you," were her last words before drifting off to sleep.

❖

Joanne shifted closer to Shanna when she felt her arm around her pulling her closer. "Is it time to get up already?" she asked as she snuggled closer to Shanna.

"No. I just wanted to feel you next to me. I was afraid it was a dream last night. A very nice dream."

"Mm. Yes. A very nice dream indeed."

"I probably ought to check on Mom." She sat up to check the clock on her dresser.

"I'll keep the bed warm," Joanne mumbled into her pillow. She felt the bed jiggle as Shanna climbed out and decided she ought to get up, too. They had work to do to get ready to head home. At least she'd be heading home. She rolled to her back and stared at the ceiling for a moment. As much as she wanted to get home and assess the damage, she refused to believe she'd have to leave Shanna behind. She took a deep breath and pushed aside the fear. Shanna had offered to help her drive home so they'd work it out somehow. After last night, she couldn't imagine anything else. She rolled out of bed and hurried to dress before heading to find Shanna.

She found Betty seated on the couch watching TV and sipping a cup of coffee. "Good morning. How're you feeling?" she asked.

"I'm much better. Thank you for asking. I think I needed a lot of rest after the stress of everything." Betty patted the seat next to her. "Care to sit and obsess with me?"

"I'm going to get a cup of coffee first." She went to the kitchen and slid her arms around Shanna. "Did you sleep well?" she asked and kissed her neck.

"I did. How about you?"

"Yep. You did an excellent job of knocking me out."

"Good. I'll have to practice more so I can get even better at it." She grinned. "I'm making the last of the pancakes, scrambled eggs, and bacon."

Joanne poured herself a cup of coffee, kissed Shanna's cheek, and went to the living room. "Anything new about the hurricane?"

"Just news coverage of the cleanup. It's a mess. I think we'll have quite a bit to do when we get there." Betty took a drink of coffee.

"It'll be okay." Joanne patted Betty's leg. "Let's not get too worried before we even see the situation."

"Breakfast anyone?" Shanna called from the kitchen.

Joanne followed Betty to the kitchen table. "Thanks for making this." She dished food on her plate and poured syrup on her pancakes.

"You're welcome. I'm on track to use up anything perishable before we head to Florida."

"Good idea. We can start packing the car." Betty smiled.

Joanne understood Betty's need to get home since her own worries began when she remembered the squatters she'd had to deal with. "Do you think squatters would try to move in after a hurricane?"

"Don't worry about it, Joanne. We'll kick them out on their butts if they've tried to move in." Shanna grinned.

Joanne chuckled. It felt good to have someone on her side. She picked up her phone and called her local police department. "Their recorded message was that the evacuation order had been lifted and they were allowing residents access to certain areas. Ours is one of them on their list, Betty." She smiled.

"Very good!" Betty toasted with her coffee cup. After breakfast, I'll start getting organized."

Joanne enjoyed seeing Betty animated. She looked forward to getting back to her house she'd only had for a few days before the evacuation, but Betty obviously had deep roots in hers. She had history with her deceased husband and memories of a life she enjoyed. Being uprooted for a month seemed a long time for her. "I'll start as well, but I'm going to relax and enjoy my coffee first."

"I'll join you, Joanne." Shanna filled her cup and settled next to her on the couch. "Let me know if you need any help packing, or anything." She grinned.

"I will. Thank you." Joanne leaned on her shoulder. "Will you be okay leaving pretty soon?"

"I will. I have a manual to work on, but I can take it with me. It's one of the perks of working from home. As long as I meet my deadline, I'm good."

"Great." She set her cup on the coffee table and leaned to kiss Shanna.

"Hmm. I'll definitely make it work."

Joanne finished her coffee and stood. "I'm going to organize a little, too." She went to her bedroom and reviewed the closet. She hadn't used all the clothes she'd brought and the ones she did were washed and folded or hung on hangers. It wouldn't take her long to pack. She went back to her seat next to Shanna where she wanted to be for as long as she had left. "It won't take me long to pack." She snuggled next to Shanna enjoying her body heat. "This is nice."

"It is." Shanna kissed her softly. "That is even nicer."

"Would you please check the gas gauge in my car, Joanne?" Betty called from her bedroom.

"I will, Betty." Joanne kissed Shanna and went to the garage. "Full tank!" She went to Betty's room to be sure she heard her.

"Thank you, honey. I couldn't remember if we filled it when we got here."

Joanne returned to the now empty couch.

Shanna returned from the kitchen carrying two full cups of coffee. "Mom still packing?"

"I'm not sure she's packing or just organizing."

"Sounds scary to me." Shanna sat and sipped her coffee.

"Thank you, again, for helping with the drive home. I think Betty will be more relaxed."

"No problem. I'll miss you," Shanna said softly.

"You're coming with us, and you can stay as long as you like." Joanne turned and cradled her face in her hands and kissed her. "I'd like you to stay a very long time."

"Okay, you two. This isn't the last time you'll see each other. It's the beginning, not the end." Betty sat next to them on the couch. "I'm all packed and ready to go, but you let me know when we leave, Shanna. You're the one with the job." Betty took a sip of coffee and turned to Joanne before speaking again. "I never really cared for the way Paul treated Shanna. I think she tried to shield me from how unhappy she was. I see her smile now, and I believe it has something to do with you. Her happiness is very important to me, and if it's because of you in her life, I welcome you with open arms." Betty sighed and took another drink of coffee.

CHAPTER TWENTY

I can work from anywhere as long as I have an Internet connection." Shanna slipped her arm around Joanne and sat for a minute to gather her thoughts. It felt good to be able to relax with Joanne in front of her mother. She could give up wrestling with how she was going to tell her about their growing relationship, but she wasn't fooling herself into thinking it would be easy for them living so far apart. She shook off her spinning thoughts and made her call.

Shanna grinned as she went back to the couch to deliver the news. "Good news." She settled next to Joanne. "I've got an extension on the due date for the manuals I'm working on."

"That's great, honey. I hope there isn't too much damage from the hurricane," Betty muttered.

"Me, too." Joanne patted Betty's hand. "Whatever it is, we'll deal with it. I'll help however I can. So, when do we leave?" Joanne asked.

"I'm ready," Betty said.

"I can be by tomorrow," Joanne said.

"Okay. How does tomorrow sound?"

"Good," Betty and Joanne replied together.

Shanna reviewed her latest finished manual. When she was satisfied it was in order, she emailed it to the company she worked for, and went shopping for supplies for their trip. She mentally reviewed her list as she shopped, and wished she'd brought Joanne with her.

"I'm back," she called out when she got home.

"Everything go smoothly?" her mother asked.

"Yes. I'm all set. I picked up a few snacks for the road." She set everything on the kitchen table.

"Looks good, honey. Thanks for picking it all up. Joanne's in her room packing." Betty smirked. "I imagine you're wondering."

"Thanks, Mom." Shanna hugged her before going to find Joanne.

"Glad you're back." Joanne kissed her quickly.

"I got us snacks for the road." Shanna stroked her cheek and smiled when Joanne leaned into her touch. "I guess I'll go pack." She went to her room and pulled out her suitcase but before packing anything, she returned to the kitchen. She sorted through her refrigerator and mentally planned dinner. Anything left over they could take with them. She returned to her room to finish packing. She rolled her suitcase to set by the door and went to check on her mom. "Do you need anything, Mom?"

"I'm good, honey. I'm all packed and just watching the news." Betty patted the seat next to her on the couch and Shanna sat.

"Anything new?" she asked.

"No. Just the ongoing cleanup."

"I've checked our food supply and we have dinner set and supplies to use up by tomorrow."

"We can pack a cooler and take leftovers with us. I'm getting a cup of coffee. Would you like one?" Betty asked as she rose to go to the kitchen.

"Thanks, Mom."

"Hey. Am I missing the party?" Joanne sat next to Shanna.

"Mom's getting us coffee."

"I'll go help." Joanne kissed Shanna quickly before leaving.

Joanne and Betty returned with coffee for all of them. "We can relax for a day." Betty lifted her cup for a toast.

"Sounds good to me." Joanne gently clinked her cup against Betty's. "It'll be a long ride home. Let's enjoy our quiet time."

"I have a good movie." Shanna pulled a DVD out of a drawer. *"Don't Look Up."* She loaded the movie in her player and relaxed back on the couch. She smiled at her mother's enthusiasm when the movie ended.

"That was a good movie. Thank you for sharing it with us," Joanne said. "More coffee?"

"Not me, thanks," Betty said.

"No. I'm good." Shanna smiled.

Joanne took their empty cups to the kitchen and washed them before going back to the living room. She turned on the TV to catch up on the situation in Florida. "You know. We ought to take some tools and maybe a rake with us. Some of those roads still look blocked. I imagine the expressway and main roads were the first to be cleared."

"Good idea." Shanna pulled a pad of paper and a pen out of a drawer and made a note. "Anything else we think of we'll write down." Shanna placed the paper and pen on the table.

Joanne picked it up and wrote a note. "Gasoline. I read somewhere that during one of the previous hurricanes gas stations were damaged and it was hard to find gas for cars."

"I don't think the authorities would have given us an all clear to return if it was impassible. We'll make a plan to not let the tank get less than half empty." She wrote the note on the paper.

Betty sighed loudly.

"It'll be okay, Mom. We'll get you home safely." Shanna pulled her into a hug.

"I'll make us some tea," Joanne said.

"That would be great. Thank you." Shanna hoped tea would relax her mother and herself. The upcoming trip was weighing on her mind. She wanted her mother to get home safely and she was happy to make sure she did, but the trip looked like it would be a challenge.

"Are you okay?" Joanne asked and placed her hand on her shoulder.

"I am. I'm just a little nervous about the trip." She leaned into Joanne's touch.

"It'll be okay. We may need to plan a longer timeframe, though. I'm guessing it'll take much longer to get back than it did to get here."

"I think you're right." Shanna stood. "I'm going to get dinner started."

"I'll help." Joanne said.

"We'll finish any leftovers tonight. Is that okay with you?"

"Can I help with anything?" Betty asked.

"Leftovers okay with you?" Shanna asked.

"Perfect."

Shanna took all the perishables out of the refrigerator and came up with a large salad and leftover chicken. "We'll have the rest for breakfast tomorrow before we leave."

"So, we're leaving tomorrow?" Betty asked.

"I think it would be better to give us more time."

"I'm ready. Tomorrow is fine with me."

Shanna and Joanne cleaned up the kitchen after dinner. "I think we're good," Shanna said. "I'm going to boil water for tea."

"Sounds good," Joanne and Betty said together.

Shanna made their tea and packed a few items in a cooler to take with them before joining them on the couch. "Anything new?"

"No. We'll probably be on the road longer than before, but it looks like they're making progress opening the roads," Betty sipped her tea as she spoke.

Shanna checked her art studio before she closed the door and locked it.

"Everything okay?" Joanne asked.

"Yes. I think we're good to go tomorrow." Shanna took her hands and pulled her into a kiss. "I miss this. Stay with me again tonight?"

Joanne smiled. "Just try to get rid of me."

"Hey, you two. The special hurricane coverage is starting," Betty called from the living room.

Shanna took Joanne's hand and led her to the couch. "Okay. Let's see what's happening." She enjoyed her tea and the heat from Joanne's body next to her while Betty watched the news intently. Her mind raced with plans. They needed to load the car and leave room for the three of them. "Make sure your phones are fully charged," she said.

"Yes, ma'am," Betty said and grinned.

"Sorry, Mom. My mind is on overload. We'll need water for drinking and the power might be out. We'll pick up bags of ice on the way."

"Sweetheart?" Joanne whispered. "Try to relax. We'll be okay." She took her hand and held it.

Shanna watched the coverage on TV and relaxed with Joanne next to her. The endearment she'd used was not lost on her, and she liked it. "Is it okay with you two if we leave at daylight?"

"Sounds good to me," Betty said.

"Sure. It'll give us a full day of light to drive in," Joanne said.

"Good night, Mom." Shanna kissed her mother's cheek before she went to bed.

"Good night, Betty." Joanne hugged her.

Shanna slid into bed and pulled Joanne close. "I'm sorry I was obsessing earlier."

"No problem." Joanne kissed her.

Shanna snuggled into her arms. "I'm a planner. I like to know what, when, how, and why I'm going to do something."

"I have an idea about something you can do." Joanne kissed her again, took her hand, and placed it on her breast.

❖

Shanna woke the next morning on the verge of a raging orgasm. She writhed in Joanne's arms and buried her moans on her shoulder. "Oh, my." She shivered.

"I like waking up with you." Joanne kissed her.

"Yeah. Me too. I suppose we should get up and get ready to leave." She pulled Joanne closer.

"Betty will be anxious." Joanne sat up and got out of bed pulling Shanna with her.

"You two awake yet?" Betty called from the living room.

"We are," Joanne called. "We'll be right out."

Shanna kissed Joanne and went to the kitchen to make coffee. "It's made, honey." Betty smiled.

"Thanks, Mom." Shanna retrieved two cups and filled them. She added a small amount of milk to one. Just the way Joanne liked it. "We'll be ready to leave soon." She took the cup to the bedroom and handed it to Joanne.

"Thank you." Joanne took a sip. "I guess we better hurry to keep up with Betty." She grinned.

CHAPTER TWENTY-ONE

I'm ready," Joanne called from her bedroom and rolled her suitcase to their designated staging area of the living room. Betty had suggested they organize everything they were taking in one spot. "It looks like we're almost ready. Anyone need a cup of coffee?"

She found Shanna standing at the kitchen counter waiting for the coffee to finish brewing. "It's almost done." Shanna kissed her quickly. "Mom is probably in the living room pacing."

"She seemed calm enough when I rolled my suitcase out there."

"Good. I'm filling a thermos with coffee for the road." She filled the thermos and poured a cup for Joanne.

"Thank you. I'm going to take a quick shower before we leave." She kissed Shanna quickly and left. Joanne took a last look around the room after her shower to be sure she wasn't leaving anything behind, packed her small overnight bag, and returned to the kitchen.

"I'm all ready to go." Betty stood by the door.

"Come and sit for a minute." Joanne took her hand and gently led her to the couch.

"I'm sorry, dear. I don't mean to be anxious, but I am."

"I know, Betty. Take a breath and finish your coffee. We'll be leaving soon."

"I need to tell you something." Betty took her hand and held it in her lap. "My daughter has been living a life she believed I wanted for her. She was miserable most of the time with Paul, but stayed with him for me. I need to tell you that I've never seen her so happy since you've come into her life. I thank you for that."

Joanne hugged Betty. "Thank you for telling me that. I have strong feelings for Shanna. Feelings that I've never had for anyone. She's an amazing woman and I hope to be in her life for a very long time, but I hope my relationship with Shanna doesn't change our friendship because I care about you."

"I know, honey. I'm happy for you both and trust that you won't hurt her." Betty hugged her and stood. "Now let's get the heck out of here and see if we have homes left to go to."

Joanne followed Shanna to her mother's car and helped load their suitcases in the trunk. "Looks like we've got plenty of room for supplies."

Shanna nodded. "Help me carry them?"

"Of course." Joanne grabbed a cooler Shanna filled with perishables from the refrigerator and wedged it into the trunk. She loaded the two smaller ones and closed the trunk. "We're ready for our adventure."

"I'm glad you have a GPS, Betty." Joanne had studied the paper map as they drove, and four hours into the trip, they ran into detours due to debris on the road and switched to the GPS unit. Shanna had been driving the whole time and Joanne worried about her obvious fatigue. "Let's stop at the next safe area. It's my turn to drive."

"I won't argue." Shanna pulled into a rest stop, leaned her head back, and closed her eyes. "I need to stretch my legs." Joanne and Betty followed her out of the car, stretched, and walked for a few minutes. "I'll get us a snack." Joanne retrieved three sandwiches and bottled water from the cooler. "We're making good time. Aren't we?" Joanne asked.

"We are." Betty squeezed her hand.

Joanne knew Betty was trying to keep them optimistic. She also knew the trip home would take longer than the trip to Shanna's. She took a deep breath and prepared herself to drive. Three hours later, Joanne pulled into a parking lot. "Shall we stretch a little before our last leg of the journey? She smiled in an attempt to keep their spirits up. "It doesn't look too bad here." She noted the roof torn off the building of a Publix. "I hope it doesn't get worse." She took a deep breath and expelled it.

"My turn to drive." Betty walked around the car a few times and stretched before settling into the driver's seat. "Next stop, home." Her smile looked forced.

"Let me know if you get tired, Mom. I'm good to drive again soon." Shanna squeezed her shoulder from the back seat. "They've done an excellent job of keeping the roads clear," Shanna said.

"They have. I expected it to be worse. We're not home yet though." Betty pointed to a boarded up restaurant.

"I think we're getting close." Joanne pointed to a huge sign. "That looks familiar." She felt the car bounce moments after she spoke. "What was that?"

"Sorry." Betty slowed the car and swerved around the debris in the street. "I guess we'll have obstacles to avoid for the rest of the way."

Betty turned onto their street an hour later. "Oh my. What a mess."

"Hopefully, your houses are intact." Shanna's heart ached at the scene. One house after another had missing roofs and/or windows. Carports seemed to take the brunt of the storm. Several were blown away or so mangled they lay halfway on the roof of the houses. Wood pieces, parts of roofs, garbage bins, and anything not tied down littered the street. Many cars parked in driveways were covered with a layer of dust or anything light enough to be blown around. Several sat untouched next to a house totally gone. She shuddered at the apocalyptic scene.

"Here we are." Betty pulled into her driveway and let out a breath. "It looks all in one piece." She climbed out of the car. "Or not. I think I lost my back room." She stood staring at the back of her house. "The carport is gone along with it." She wiped tears away.

Joanne climbed out of the car and looked across the street. "Mine is still standing, too. The carport's gone though." She went to the back of the car and began unloading their suitcases.

Betty took her suitcase to her front porch and returned for Shanna's. "Leave yours in the trunk, Joanne. I'll drive you to your house to unload your stuff. The street looks dangerous to walk on."

Joanne agreed and helped carry the rest of Betty's belongings into her house.

Shanna checked all her faucets to confirm she had water and turned on her lights. "Looks like you're okay with water but no electricity."

"Thank you, honey." Betty sank into her recliner. "I'm beat."

"You rest, Mom. Joanne and I will unload the car and I'll take her home." Shanna finished at her mother's and drove Joanne across the street to her house. "Weird. It looks like your side of the street has power. Mom's is out."

"Thanks for your help." Joanne kissed Shanna as soon as they stepped into her house. The inside looked untouched except for a couple of broken windows, and Joanne sent up a prayer of thanks to whatever power had saved her house. Her last connection to her parents. "My parents bought this house and hoped to retire here," she told Shanna.

"It's a nice house." Shanna followed Joanne on a tour and noted the broken windows. "We'll head to the hardware store later to get supplies and cover the windows with plastic for now. Mom's going to need to hire someone to rebuild her back room."

"It's nice having two bedrooms, so my friend Heather can stay if she visits. Betty's welcome to stay here if she needs to."

"What if I visit?" Shanna wrapped her arms around her and kissed her.

"I have a double bed." Joanne leaned into the kiss.

"I'd better go check on Mom." Shanna stepped back and turned to go.

Joanne put away the few perishables Shanna had given her. She watched the update on the hurricane and recognized how tired she was.

She woke to soft lips caressing hers. "Mm. I like waking to this." She took Shanna's hand and pulled her down on the couch. "Is your mom resting?"

"She was sound asleep when I went to check on her. I made sure she had her suitcase and some food. I'll go back and check on her later, but the electricity came on while I was there."

"Will you be able to stay with me before you go home?"

"I hope so. I'll stay with Mom for a few days to make sure she's settled in, and I'll arrange for someone to do repairs on her house. It's a little too much for me to handle."

"Sure. Let me know if I can help with anything. You wander across the street anytime you want to."

"I'm going to make dinner for Mom. Why don't you come over?"

"Just let me unpack a little and I'll be there." She pulled her against herself and kissed her.

Joanne put away her toiletries and took a shower before changing her clothes and heading to Betty's. She stopped as she stepped out of the door to check her car. The carport was nowhere to be seen, and her car looked dirty, but undamaged. She counted her blessings and continued to Betty's.

"Hello," she called from the door before going inside. Betty reclined in a very comfortable looking chair and appeared to be sound asleep. "I think a nap sounds like a great idea." Joanne settled on Betty's couch.

"Yeah. I'm pretty tired, too." Shanna set a plate of tuna sandwiches on the coffee table. "Help yourself." She gently squeezed Betty's shoulder. "Have a sandwich, Mom. Then you can go lay on your bed."

"Thank you. How's your house, Joanne?" Betty asked between bites.

"It's okay. My carport is gone and a couple of windows are broken, but the house seems solid. I'm glad the worst of the storm missed us." Joanne took a bite of sandwich and realized how hungry she was. "Thank you for the sandwich. I was hungry." She finished eating and carried her plate to the sink while Shanna followed her mother to her room. Betty didn't need anything to do when she woke up so Joanne washed the few dishes and put them away. She looked around and felt satisfied things were in order as she waited for Shanna. She hoped she'd go home with her and stay the night. What came after that, she wasn't sure.

CHAPTER TWENTY-TWO

S he's out like a light. I think the trip took more out of her than she thought it would." Shanna sat next to Joanne.

"It was pretty stressful." Joanne rested her arms on Shanna's shoulders and kissed her. "Do you need to stay with her tonight?"

"I'll check with her when she gets up. She may want to be alone back in her own house, or she may appreciate the company."

"I'd love it if you could spend the night with me."

"I'd love that, too." Shanna paused. "We'll work it out, Joanne. I really want to."

"Yeah. Me too."

Joanne kissed her and left. Shanna went through her mother's house and dusted and vacuumed after cleaning up the kitchen. She smiled at the neatly stacked plates in the drainer. Joanne was special to her. She could easily admit that to herself, but where their relationship was going was an unknown. She wanted more with her, but wasn't sure how to work that out. She pushed aside any more thoughts and checked on her mom before settling on the couch and turning on the television. Coverage of the hurricane still dominated the news so she watched for anything new. She was startled awake half an hour later and checked on her mom before going to Joanne's.

"What a nice surprise." Joanne kissed her and tugged her to the living room.

"I was hoping we could take a nap together. Mom is still asleep." Shanna smiled when Joanne took her hand and pulled her to her bedroom.

"I miss you being around." She sank into Joanne's arms and kissed her.

"Me too."

"What are we going to do?" Shanna held Joanne in her arms. "How are we going to make this work?"

"I don't know, but we will." Joanne pushed her onto her back on her bed and stretched out on top of her. "You feel so good."

"I need to make sure Mom is settled."

"Okay." Joanne rolled to her side to face Shanna. "She knows we've spent the night together. She probably wouldn't be surprised if you spent the night here. Or me with you. Would she?"

"Probably not." Shanna wondered if that was true. "Let's play it by ear. We just got here." She stopped her racing thoughts and kissed her.

❖

Shanna rolled over and looked for a clock. She remembered kissing Joanne and holding her while they made love. Now it was an hour later and Joanne lay sleeping next to her. The trip had obviously worn them out and she wondered if her mom was awake yet. She kissed Joanne lightly and got up to go check on her. She found her mom seated in her recliner reading a book.

"Hello, dear. Is Joanne settling in?"

"She is. I helped her move some debris away from her door wall. It looks like her carport was the biggest thing affected by the hurricane. Do you feel a little rested?"

"I do. That trip took a lot out of me."

"It was a long drive, and there was the stress of the unknown. You can relax now. If you need anything just ask." Shanna went outside and moved debris away from the door and in her mother's yard. Her neighbor had broken windows and a tree limb sticking out of their roof. She went to their door and called out, but it looked like the house was vacant and she hoped no one had been hurt. She returned to her mother's. "It looks like your neighbors are gone."

"They have a son in Georgia. They probably went there." She went back to reading her book. "You don't have to hang around, honey. Later, we can use up all the leftovers we brought. Go ask Joanne to join us for dinner."

"I will. Do you need anything from the store? More groceries?"

"If you're going, I could use some milk and eggs."

"I'll be back soon." She kissed her mom's cheek and went back to Joanne's.

"Need anything from the grocery store?" she asked.

"I do. Let's go." Joanne kissed her before heading to the door.

Shanna helped Joanne put away her groceries when they returned and went to her mother's. "I'm back, Mom." She put her groceries away and made her a bowl of chicken noodle soup.

"It's okay if you want to stay with Joanne, honey. I can see you two care about each other, and I absolutely approve although I don't presume you need my approval."

Shanna sat next to her and took her hand. "I'm grateful you care enough to let me know how you feel. I like Joanne a lot, but I'm not sure where we're headed. I just know I like spending time with her, and she feels the same way."

"Just be careful with your heart, honey. I love you and I don't want to see you hurt. It had to be difficult with Paul and you might need time to heal from that before getting into a serious relationship."

Shanna kissed her mother's cheek. "Thank you, Mom." She sat across from her on the couch. "I've actually thought of that. I don't want to be hurt by Joanne or hurt her. We haven't made any commitments and we're taking things a day at a time. Both of us have just been through a serious upset. Fortunately, it turned out all right, but we're both exhausted. I promise I'll take the time for us both to heal."

"How'd you get so smart, honey?" Her mom smiled.

"I had you and Dad to guide me. I love you, Mom." Shanna wrapped her mother in a hug.

"I love you, too." Her mom squeezed her tightly.

"I've piled all the debris I picked up from your yard at the end of your driveway. It'll be picked up won't it?"

"Yes. On Thursday unless the storm has changed things."

"Okay. I'll go check on Joanne. We'll be back for dinner."

"Great. We're kind of used to that now, aren't we?"

"Yes, we are." She kissed her mom's cheek and left.

Shanna went back to Joanne's and called to her from the door.

"Come on in, Shanna." Joanne sat in her living room with a cup of tea. "Can I make you a cup?"

"No, thank you. I'm good. I wanted to invite you to dinner."

"What time should I be there?"

"Anytime, but I think Mom is still resting. The trip knocked her out."

Joanne looked at her watch. "We have time then." She took Shanna's hand and pulled her on top of herself and kissed her. Shanna pulled her against herself and smoothed her hand over her back under her shirt. Her skin was warm and soft. She slid her hands to her ass and pressed herself against her. Joanne writhed beneath her and they both moaned and embraced each other as they came. "You make me feel so good," Joanne breathed. "Will you stay with me?"

"I'm here."

"No. I mean stay and live with me. Your mom is right across the street. You could work here." Joanne stroked her cheek.

"Oh, Joanne…I don't know. I have a house. I don't know."

"Think about it? Please."

Shanna took a deep breath. "I'll think about it."

"Okay. I'm going to change for dinner." Joanne kissed her quickly and went to her bedroom to change.

"Thank you for inviting me to dinner, Betty." Joanne hugged her.

"We can't break the routine now." She grinned.

"Next time it's my turn to cook."

Shanna finished her meal and sipped coffee while she listened to her mom and Joanne talk. It wouldn't be awful to stay in Florida and live with her, but the niggling in her gut told her to take it slow. They'd only known each other a short time. Yes, they were good together and she had real feelings for her, but living together was a commitment she wasn't sure she was ready for. She'd just gotten rid of Paul and had settled into the serenity of solitary life. She wasn't sure she knew how to share her life with anyone.

"What do you think, honey?"

Shanna blinked. She hadn't heard her mother's question. "Sorry, what?"

"What do you think about you staying with me for a few weeks?"

Shanna felt pressured, but she was certain that wasn't what her mother intended. She actually had considered staying a while with her mother. She could work from here and help her mother and her neighbors recover from the hurricane damage. And she didn't want to leave Joanne. "I think that might be a very good idea." She grinned when her mother clapped and Joanne smiled. She rose to make hot chocolate for them and relaxed in her mother's living room.

"This feels familiar." Joanne chuckled.

"It's nice." Betty sipped from her cup.

"It is nice," Shanna agreed.

"Would you two like to go to the water with me tomorrow?" Joanne asked.

"If we can get through the stuff all over the street."

"Let's try." Betty looked excited. "I haven't been to the shore in years."

"Okay. We'll go right after breakfast." Shanna lifted her cup in a toast.

CHAPTER TWENTY-THREE

T hanks for walking me home. Come in with me?" Joanne raised their joined hands and kissed Shanna's fingers.

"Of course. I'd like to stay with you."

"I hoped you would. Betty won't mind will she?"

"I don't think so. I think she probably presumes I will."

Joanne unpacked the grocery bags when they returned from the store. The choices had been limited due to everyone shopping after the hurricane. "We can come back in a few days and hope they've restocked."

"It's too bad they lost power there. Mom wanted a couple of chickens for her freezer." Shanna picked out what she could find from her mother's list.

"This will have to do for now." Joanne put away what she had. "I'd like to cuddle on the couch, but do you think your mom needs company?"

"Let's take her the few items I bought for her and see how she feels."

"Okay. First, I need this." She cupped Shanna's face and kissed her.

"I needed that, too." Shanna took Joanne's hand and led her across the street to Betty's.

"Hi, Mom," Shanna called from the doorway. "We're back from the store."

"Come on in, you two. I have hot tea waiting."

Joanne smiled at the familiar routine. They'd be seated on her couch soon, sipping tea and watching the television. "Thank you for the tea, Betty."

"The grocery store pickings were pretty slim. Everyone is trying to refill their freezers and refrigerators. I'll go back in a few days to look for your chicken." Shanna sat next to Joanne and rested her arm around her shoulders.

"I'm relieved to see something on TV besides a dangerous hurricane approaching."

"Yeah, but now it's all about the cleanup." Joanne pointed to the television. "That's the next street over from us. It's nearly blocked."

"We'll check things out tomorrow when we go to the water." Betty leaned back on the couch and drank her tea.

Joanne relaxed as she leaned against Shanna and watched TV with Betty. When she'd moved to Florida, she worried about making friends and settling into a home so far away from everything she was familiar with. Now she felt gratitude for her good fortune to have found good friends and possibly love. She knew she wanted more with Shanna, and hoped they could have time together to see where their relationship would go. She sent a silent prayer to her deceased parents to thank them for leaving her the house. "I'm grateful that you two are in my life. I didn't have any idea what I'd find in Florida and discovered my parents left me a very nice house. Now I have friends to go with that house."

"You do have friends. And I'm grateful that you're here to be my friend." Betty toasted with her cup.

Joanne snuggled closer to Shanna to enjoy the warmth from her body, and was grateful when she hugged her tighter. She fought her growing fatigue and forced herself not to yawn. "Are you two as tired as I am?"

Betty answered first. "I can hardly keep my eyes open."

Shanna squeezed her and stood. "It's time for all of us to get some rest." She kissed Betty's cheek. "Good night, Mom. Sleep well."

Joanne took Shanna's hand as they walked across the street to her house. "I'm glad you're coming home with me."

"I hoped you'd want me to. Mom's lived alone since my dad died, and she'd appreciate me staying with her. I'll plan on doing that a few days while I'm here."

"I'll miss you, but that's a good idea. I plan to invite her for dinner tomorrow."

"There's still quite a bit of cleanup to do on your street." Shanna pointed to parts of carports, roofs, and windows littering the street. "I'll go house-to-house tomorrow and check their yards."

"Good idea. I'll help you. In fact, I'll check on the people, too. Make sure nobody is trapped in their house or needs anything." Joanne looked at her watch. "Would you mind if we started now? Tomorrow may be too late for some people. Let's get paper and pencil so we can keep track of what they might need."

Shanna kissed her. "I think that's a good idea. I'll start on Mom's side of the street and you start on yours."

Joanne retrieved a few garbage bags for Shanna and herself before heading to the first house. She cleaned up their yard and cleared their driveway so they could get their car out before knocking on their door and noting any groceries they might need. She repeated the process with each subsequent house until she reached the end of the street.

"I think we got everyone." Shanna showed her the list she'd made.

"I think so, too. Let's go home and we can shop for them tomorrow. I'm ready to fall into bed."

Joanne woke the next morning to the smell of cooking bacon. She followed the scent to the kitchen and wrapped her arms around Shanna from behind. "Thank you for cooking." She nuzzled her neck.

"Keep doing that, and I'm done cooking."

"Okay." Joanne stepped away and retrieved plates and silverware. "I'll save it for later." She made them each a cup of coffee and sat at her small kitchen table. "Do we have enough to invite your mom to breakfast?"

"Sure. Good idea."

Joanne called Betty and invited her. "She'll be over in five minutes." She poured another cup of coffee and set it across from her on the table.

"Hello," Betty called from the door before entering the house. "It smells great in here."

"Come join us." Joanne retrieved another chair, plate, and silverware.

"Thank you for the invitation. I was going to have cottage cheese with blueberries. This is wonderful."

"You can thank Shanna. I'm afraid cottage cheese and blueberries is more like what I'd come up with for breakfast. Or Cream of Wheat." She grinned.

"I remember. I guess Shanna is a good influence on you." Betty took her hand and squeezed gently. "I'm glad you came into her life."

"Thank you, Betty. I'm very glad, too. We're going shopping today for some of the neighbors. Do you need anything?"

"I'll make a list, honey. It's nice of you two to help out. Gladys across the street can't drive. She's probably been stuck in her house for days." She sipped her coffee and set her cup down before continuing. "I'm going to start a neighborhood watch. I bet there are others who'd want to help, too."

"I think that's a great idea, Mom. Neighbors helping neighbors is a blessing for many."

"Perfect! Thank you, Shanna. That's the name of my new organization. I'll make up flyers and distribute them next week." She stood and took her empty plate and cup to the sink. "I'll see you two later. Come to dinner tonight?"

"We'll be there." Joanne smiled at Betty's enthusiasm. "Thanks for making breakfast," Joanne murmured against the back of Shanna's neck after Betty left.

"We have a lot of shopping to do today," Shanna said quietly as she pulled Joanne closer.

"We do." Joanne kept up her nuzzling. "Store's open all day."

❖

"I think we've got everything," Shanna said when they returned from the store and sorted the items they'd bought. "We can deliver most of it before going to Mom's for dinner and then finish later."

"Sounds good." Joanne made sure each group of items had a note attached as to who it belonged to. "Shall I start delivering these?"

"Sure. I'll get the next bunch."

Joanne carried the first group of items to the first neighbor on their list and realized this was not going to be a quick event. The neighbor insisted she come in and have a cup of coffee, and before she could leave she went through a number of thank you hugs and invitations to come back to visit. She promised she would and was finally allowed to leave.

"How're your deliveries going?" she asked Shanna as she collected items for the next group.

"Wow. I had no idea these people were so starved for visitors. It's nice though. It makes me realize what's important. They need their supplies, but they need human contact and interaction too."

"Yeah. I can understand that, but we probably won't get everything delivered today at this rate."

"Maybe. We can finish tomorrow. Let's get all the perishables delivered and the rest we can do later or even tomorrow."

Joanne put all the leftover neighbor's items in her extra bedroom for delivery the next day before changing and waiting for Shanna.

"Whew. I think we're done for the day." Shanna kissed her lightly and went to change her clothes. "I hope Mom's ready for us. I'm starving."

"Me too." Joanne retrieved two bottles of water and handed one to Shanna. "I'm glad we did that today. The people I talked to were so grateful it brought tears to my eyes. A few even offered me money." She sighed.

"Yeah. Me too. I'm glad we could help them. A hurricane is an awful thing to live through and then they have the expense of replacing food and things they lost."

"That reminds me, I have to call my boss tomorrow. I hope I still have a job." Joanne frowned. "I hope the bank is still standing."

CHAPTER TWENTY-FOUR

"Hi, Mom. We're here," Shanna said as she and Joanne arrived.

"Come on in, you two. Dinner will be ready soon." Betty offered them each a glass of wine.

"Thank you, Betty, but I don't drink alcohol." Joanne lifted her bottle of water she'd brought.

Shanna also refused the wine in favor of water.

"Well, I'm having one." Betty settled on the couch. "How did the shopping for the neighborhood go today?"

"It went well. We finished our street and tomorrow we'll do the next one. Your neighbors are great people."

Betty laughed. "They are. Did they invite you in for tea or coffee? Did they talk your ears off? And they probably offered to pay you, didn't they?"

"Yes, all of the above." Shanna laughed. "We accepted some money for the groceries, but we're just glad we could help them."

"It was fun to meet so many of them since they're my neighbors now, too," Joanne said.

"Maybe, when you're settled in, you can help me with my neighbors helping neighbors endeavor."

"I'd like that," Joanne said.

"Dinner's ready." Betty put a plate of meatloaf on the table along with a huge salad.

"Thanks, Mom. This looks great."

"Yeah. Thank you, Betty. We've been too busy to eat since breakfast."

"How was the grocery store today?" Betty asked.

"It was better stocked, but still not full," Shanna said.

"We pretty much found what we needed for people though," Joanne said between bites.

"I'm waiting until next week to go. It's quite a social event on Saturday afternoon. Many of our neighbors gather there and the gossip flows. It's fun."

"I'll have to remember that," Joanne said.

"We'll have to make up some juicy gossip for you." Shanna smiled.

Joanne chuckled. "I hate gossip."

"Me too, but it sounds like it's a Saturday afternoon pastime around here." Shanna took her hand. "I'll help you clean up while Mom relaxes."

"You don't have to do that, honey." Her mom stood.

"You did the cooking. We do the cleaning up." Joanne smiled.

"I won't argue. By the way. The tea is in the cupboard above the sink." Betty sat on the couch and rested her feet on the coffee table. "I'm so glad you two are getting along. I worried that it might get hard for you away from home, Shanna. When do you have to go back to work?"

"I brought my laptop and the manuals I have to finish. I can work from here as long as there's an Internet connection. I kind of like it here."

"I like having you so close, honey, and I'm certain Joanne does, too."

Joanne set two cups of tea on the table and took Shanna's hand. "I do. Very much."

Shanna hadn't thought much about returning to her life five hundred miles away. The few days spent with Joanne had been wonderful. It felt right being with her, but her house stood vacant and most of her clothes were still there. She'd have to make a decision soon. She relaxed on the couch between her mom and Joanne and postponed thoughts of work.

"Tomorrow I'm going to call someone about replacing my carport and my back room. I'll let you know what they say." Betty sipped her tea.

"Thanks, Betty. I hope I can afford to do that. It was nice having that covered outside area."

Shanna rested her arm around Joanne and pulled her close. She'd make sure Joanne had a new carport before she left.

"Shall we go home and review our shopping list for tomorrow?" Joanne asked.

"Sounds good. Let us know if you need anything, Mom." Shanna stood and stretched. "Thank you for dinner." She kissed her mother's cheek before taking Joanne's hand and leading her to the door.

"Could I talk to you for a minute before you go, honey?"

"Sure, Mom." She kissed Joanne lightly. "I'll be right out."

"I just wanted to talk for a minute." She took a breath before continuing. "When I first met Joanne, she was shy and seemed fearful of people. I know she was hurt by an ex-lover and had recently lost her parents. I can see you two are growing close, and I wanted to ask you to be careful with her heart, as well as your own."

"Thank you, Mom. Joanne hasn't opened up to me yet about whatever she's holding in, but I care about her, and I can be patient." She kissed her mother's cheek. "I'll be careful."

"I'm a little tired from the long day," Joanne said when they returned to her living room. "Would you like another cup of tea?"

"No, thank you. Let's relax and watch TV." Shanna hoped they could find something to watch besides news about the hurricane.

Joanne settled next to her and cuddled into her when she put her arm around her. "Mm. This is nice."

"Yes, it is." Shanna mentally reviewed her mother's words to her. "So, you're okay with me here aren't you?"

"Sweetheart. I love that you're here with me. I hope you're happy here." Joanne sat forward and frowned.

"I am. It's just that it wasn't planned. We escaped the hurricane and things are settling down. I'm not sure when I'll have to go back to my house, but I'll miss you." She leaned and kissed Joanne.

Joanne was quiet for so long, Shanna took her hand and kissed it. "What?"

"I'll miss you, too, if you leave."

"We'll work it out."

Joanne rested her head on her shoulder and Shanna pulled her close. "We have to."

Shanna considered her mother's words again. "When do you have to go back to work?"

"I'll call the bank tomorrow and see what the situation is." Joanne sighed. "It'll have to be pretty soon if I plan to buy a new carport." After she spoke, she remembered the homeowner's insurance papers she'd found along with the deed to her house. "I forgot about the house insurance. It may cover the replacement of the carport."

"I never asked you if you have any family back in Michigan."

"No. My parents were my only family. I told you I grew up in foster care."

"You did."

"My parents adopted me when I was sixteen. I do have a family friend. Heather. She's also my therapist."

"Therapist?"

"I'm going to make a cup of tea. You want one?"

"Okay. Thanks." Shanna sensed Joanne's nervousness. Whatever she was about to tell her was important. She followed her into the kitchen and wrapped her arms around her from behind. She kissed her neck and held her hand. "You don't have to tell me if you don't want to."

"I do want to tell you. And I want to hear all about you. You're very important to me, Shanna."

"And you are very important to me, too. Come back to the couch."

Joanne settled next to her but didn't cuddle like she usually did. "Have you ever heard of fetal alcohol syndrome?"

"No." Shanna sensed Joanne was disclosing something important and held her gaze.

"It's a condition that affects the fetus when the mother drinks alcohol while pregnant like mine did. My parents took a big chance adopting me. I was an out-of-control teen. They took me to Heather, my therapist, to be evaluated, and I was diagnosed with the condition. There's no cure, but I can manage my life now that I know about it. I'll never be able to drink alcohol and I have memory issues, but I can take care of myself and live a full life."

Shanna kissed her gently. "Thank you for telling me."

"I wanted you to know. I want you to know me, and I want to know you. All of you. Your hopes and dreams for the future." Joanne snuggled into her then and sighed.

"You already know my mom, so that's a start. I grew up in Illinois and got my teaching degree at Northwestern University. I met and married Paul when I was twenty-five. You know how that turned out. I began teaching in Illinois as soon as I graduated and hated it, so I used what I learned and began editing for an auto company. And that's about it for me."

"And your hopes for the future?"

Shanna pulled Joanne close. "They definitely include you." Then she kissed her. "Let's go to bed and put each other to sleep." Shanna took Joanne's hand and led her to the bedroom.

Shanna considered everything Joanne had told her as she held her in her arms after they made love. She was a brave woman to have grown up with her disability and made a life for herself as an independent adult. Her growing feelings for Joanne were only strengthened by Joanne's disclosure.

CHAPTER TWENTY-FIVE

Shanna rolled over and pulled Joanne close. "I like waking up with you," she whispered and kissed her bare shoulder.

"Mm. Me too," Joanne mumbled. "But do we have to get up yet?"

"Nope." She nestled closer to Joanne under the covers. She woke half an hour later and kissed Joanne quickly before getting out of bed.

She searched the refrigerator for breakfast food and made a note to buy more eggs and bacon. She took out a pan and set it on the stove. She'd cook when Joanne got up. She poured herself a glass of orange juice and sat to watch the morning news on TV.

"Hey there." Joanne settled next to her.

"Morning, sweetie. Would you like a glass?" She held up her orange juice.

"No, thank you. I'll have a cup of coffee soon." Joanne set up the coffee maker and sat next to Shanna. "Did you sleep okay?"

"I did. How about you?" Shanna sipped her orange juice.

"Oh yes. I love sleeping with you." Joanne went to get herself a cup of coffee and returned with two. "I brought you a cup."

"Thank you." Shanna set her orange juice aside. ..."I want to tell you something." Joanne took a second to organize her thoughts. "I got nervous last night after I told you about my disability. I'm scared you're going to leave me." Joanne held back her tears. It was hard enough admitting her fears without turning into a blubbering mess.

"Oh, Joanne." Shanna pulled her into her arms. "You don't need to worry about me leaving because you have to deal with something beyond your control. I want to be here for you. If you need any help, I want to be the one you turn to."

"Thank you. I'm sorry to be a baby about it, but I care about you so much and I don't want to lose you."

"I may have to return home to settle some things, but I hope you want me to come back."

"I do. I want you here with me." Joanne pulled her against herself. "Is that selfish? You have a house."

"We'll work it out, sweetheart."

Joanne relaxed. She'd convinced herself Shanna was leaving and she'd never see her again, so she replayed her words over in her mind. Shanna cared about her and she'd come back to her. She couldn't allow herself to believe anything different.

"I'm going to get in the shower," Shanna said. "Join me?"

Joanne tossed her pajamas onto the bed and strode naked to the bathroom. "Absolutely." She followed Shanna into the shower and pressed herself against her back as she reached around her and covered her breasts with soapy hands. She spread her fingers and gently squeezed her hardened nipples as she spread soap over her breasts. Shanna's nipples tickled her palms as she slid her hands over them. She skimmed her hands down to her belly and massaged gently with soapy fingers.

Shanna turned in her arms and gasped as their breasts met and she glided them against Joanne's. "I'm not sure I can stand much longer."

"Let's go back to bed." Joanne stepped out of the shower, grabbed a towel, and pulled Shanna out.

"We're supposed to go back to the store this morning." Shanna writhed beneath Joanne as she spoke.

"We will. First things first." Joanne scooted down Shanna's body until she could reach her with her mouth. She slowly parted her and flicked her clit with her tongue. Shanna moaned and lifted her hips in a silent plea. Joanne gently sucked until it hardened to a knot. She sucked and flicked while keeping up with Shanna's thrusting hips. She whimpered when Shanna thrust hard, shuddered, and came.

"Oh my God." Shanna's chest rose and fell as she gasped. "Baby, that was amazing."

"I'm glad I remembered what to do. It's been a long time." Joanne smiled in relief.

"I think it's my turn now." Shanna rolled over and kissed her.

"We should probably get to the store. We can continue this later."

Shanna slipped her hand between them and glided a finger into Joanne's wetness. "Or we can finish it now," she said. "And do it again later."

Joanne had been close to coming while she was making love to Shanna so she relaxed and went with the intense feelings Shanna's touch evoked. "Oh, that's it. Yes!" Her orgasm tore through her like an electrical current igniting every cell in her body. She clung to Shanna as the ripples rolled through her and subsided. "I'm not sure I can walk." She nestled into Shanna and held her tight.

She blinked awake twenty minutes later and looked at the clock. She got up to use the bathroom and returned to remind Shanna of their shopping trip.

"Hmm. Okay." Shanna rolled over and closed her eyes.

Joanne went through the notes they had from the neighbors and decided she could probably get all they needed on her own. She'd miss sharing the event with Shanna, but she didn't have the heart to wake her when she looked so peaceful. She left her a love note and let her know she was going to the store before she left.

❖

Joanne walked down every aisle in the store to find items on her lists. She filled a whole cart, checked out, and loaded everything into her car before heading home. Shanna would help her distribute the supplies later. She hoped she'd be awake when she got home.

She had all the items sorted and in bags by the time Shanna shuffled into the kitchen looking sleepy.

"Sorry I conked out on you." Shanna looked at all the bags placed around the room. "You've been busy."

"I think we're done. All we have to do is distribute the bags."

"I can help with that, at least." Shanna got dressed and returned looking more awake. "Let's get to it."

Joanne plopped onto her couch when they returned from their task. "Whew. That was a lot of walking."

"Yes, it was, but it seemed silly to drive to one house, get out, drive to the next house, and get out, and so on and so on. Now we're done."

"Your mom was happy that we stopped by. Let's invite her for dinner tomorrow."

"Sounds good." Shanna turned on the TV.

"Do you feel all right?" Joanne asked.

"I do. Why?"

"You fell asleep earlier, and I couldn't wake you up."

"You knocked me out, and I think the stress of the hurricane and the drive got to me. I finally relaxed and felt safe enough to sleep. Like I said. You knocked me out."

Joanne accepted Shanna's explanation, grateful it alleviated her concern. "I'll have to be gentler in the future." She smiled.

"Maybe we should go practice." Shanna rested her hands on Joanne's hips and kissed her.

Shanna's phone interrupted their intended lovemaking. "Hi, Mom." Shanna kept one arm around Joanne as she listened to her mother. "Thanks, Mom. I'll tell Joanne."

"Tell me what?" It sounded like they wouldn't be going back to bed.

"Mom wants us to come over for lunch."

"Right now?"

"She says the lasagna is just coming out of the oven." Shanna shrugged.

"I guess we'll postpone our practice session until tonight." Joanne kissed her quickly and took her hand to walk across the street.

"Come on in, you two," Betty called from the kitchen when they arrived.

"Thank you for inviting us," Joanne said.

"I miss you both. I guess I got used to you being around, and I wanted to do something to thank you for your help when I got sick."

"You'd have done the same thing." Shanna kissed her mother's cheek.

"I wanted to ask you something today." Betty hesitated. "My friend June came over last night to ask for some help, and I'm hoping you'll offer to join me."

"Help with what, Mom?"

Betty set a few pictures on the table in front of them. "Her house has substantial damage from the hurricane. She's been widowed for years and can't afford to hire the company that's been doing restoration work in the area. I walked home with her to see what needed to be done, and I think between the three of us, we can fix most things for her."

"We can certainly go take a look." Joanne glanced at Shanna after looking at the pictures.

"Sure we can." Shanna squeezed Joanne's hand.

"Great. We'll go right after lunch." Betty dished pieces of lasagna on three plates and sat at the table.

Joanne tried not to think about what repairs June's house might need that didn't show up in the pictures. She held Shanna's hand as they followed Betty to June's after lunch.

"She's lost her carport, too." Joanne looked up and down the street and realized most driveways were open. She followed Shanna as she walked around the outside of June's house and assessed the damage. Her bedroom window was shattered and half of the shingles on her roof were missing. "We can probably cover her broken window until it's replaced."

"Yeah. We'll have to find a roofer to replace the shingles." Shanna picked up a piece from the ground. "Is everything okay inside, June?" she asked.

June clasped her hands and held them to her chest. "I can't find Wilber." Tears streamed down her cheeks.

Betty put her arm around her and pulled her close. "We'll find him. He's probably just scared and hiding. Wilber is her cat. She's had him since he was a kitten."

Joanne took Shanna's hand and squeezed gently. "Can we help her look for him? Maybe he's hiding under some of this debris."

"We'll search the whole area, June. We'll do our best to find him." Betty hugged her.

"Let's split up and cover the whole back area. Be careful not to trip on anything." Shanna began searching on one side of the yard.

Joanne turned over everything she could move as she searched along the perimeter of the yard. "Is the inside of her house livable?" she asked Betty.

"It is except the broken window is right above her bed. Can we put cardboard or something over it?"

"Yes, we can. I have some plastic at home, too. That will be better if it rains." Joanne continued her searching until she got to the back of the yard. "I'll go home and get the plastic now." She told Shanna her plan and went home. She returned with the plastic and tape and quickly sealed the window for June. She walked through the rest of the house to verify it was secure before going back outside. "It looks like there's no damage inside. June should be safe. I'll be back with some garbage bags." Joanne began to head home and stopped two houses from her when she heard a quiet mewing. She peeked behind a line of bushes and saw two green eyes staring at her. The small cat slowly crawled out from behind the bushes and rubbed on Joanne's leg. She picked him up and carried him back to June. "Wilber wants his mom." Joanne handed him to June who cradled him like a baby.

"Thank you so much." Tears still streamed down June's cheeks and Joanne hoped they were happy tears.

CHAPTER TWENTY-SIX

W hat a mess." Shanna picked up one of the garbage bags and tossed it on the pile they'd made in June's front yard. The garbage collection was scheduled for the next day and there were very few houses on the block that didn't have a pile waiting for pick up. "I'm glad your house was spared more damage," she told Joanne.

"Me too. Some of these folks have serious loss."

"Mom's fortunate, too." Shanna took a drink from her water bottle. "Would you mind if I stayed a few more days?"

"You can stay as long as you like. I believe I've told you I'd like it if you moved in with me." Joanne kissed her.

"I'd like to help my mom's neighbors if I can. I'm glad her house wasn't damaged." She finished a piece of her mother's lasagna.

"We seem to be the youngsters of the neighborhood. I'd love to help you help them." Joanne finished her piece and sipped her water. "And, I'd love it if you stayed forev—"

Shanna interrupted her. "I can stay with my mom if I'm in your way."

"God no, Shanna. I want you with me for as long as you want to stay." Joanne placed her hand over hers. "We can make the rounds of the neighborhood and help the most vulnerable first."

"Yes. Mom will have a list of the neighbors. We can canvas them and record what they need." Shanna stopped and held Joanne's gaze. "Are you sure you want to commit to this with me?"

"I want you here. With me. Of course I'll help you." Joanne pulled her into her arms and kissed her. "We have practicing to do, remember?"

"Oh. I haven't forgotten." Shanna kissed her.

"How does pizza sound for dinner?" Joanne asked.

"Great."

"Vegetarian with extra cheese okay?"

"Sounds good."

"I'll make the call."

Shanna enjoyed sharing the pizza with Joanne. She enjoyed being with her and believed Joanne felt the same but worried Joanne might get tired of her. She'd only moved to Florida a short time ago and barely had time to settle in when the hurricane chased her out of her home. Would it be fair to tie her down before she had a chance to spend time alone in her new home? They needed to talk. "I'm kind of tired from all the activity today. How about you?"

"I am a little, but it feels good to have been able to help everyone." Joanne sat on the couch and put her feet up.

Shanna settled next to her. "I like being with you." She rested her hand on her leg.

"I'm glad, because I feel the same way." Joanne kissed her. "You're thinking of leaving, aren't you?"

Shanna sat quietly for a minute considering her answer. Apparently, this was the time for their talk. "No. I'm concerned that I'm pushing you into a relationship you're not ready for."

"Oh, baby. No. You're the best thing that has ever happened to me. It's true I wasn't looking for anything when I met you, but that doesn't mean it's not right. That I'm not ready. I told you about Stacy in Michigan. She and I dated for over a year before we were physical. We slept together sometimes, but it was never like it is between us. You are my person."

"I've never felt so connected to anyone before." Shanna kissed her and sighed deeply. Right or wrong, they'd work it out together.

"Shall we see what's on the news?" Joanne picked up the remote and turned on the TV before snuggling closer to Shanna. "Thank goodness the hurricane coverage is lessening. I was getting tired of it."

"Yeah. We have firsthand knowledge of it now," Shanna said.

"I just remembered we bought ice cream today." Joanne hurried to the kitchen and returned with two bowls of ice cream.

"Thanks for remembering." Shanna took a big bite. "Let's watch something besides the news. Okay?"

"Fine with me." Joanne turned to the movie channel. "I'm going to miss watching movies in the middle of the day when I go back to work."

"When will that be?"

"Next week. My boss told me the bank sustained minor damage but not enough to close down."

"My editing for automotive manuals can be done anywhere."

"You can work from home then?"

"Yes. I like that about it most of all."

"I like the idea of you living and working here." Joanne snuggled closer to Shanna. "I have Internet service if you need it. At least I hope it still works. We'll try it later."

"I will need it, and I plan to cover the cost." Shanna picked up Joanne's hand and held it in her lap.

"I'm having a cup of tea. Would you like one?" Joanne asked.

"Sure. I've gotten used to sitting on the couch sipping tea." Shanna grinned. She watched Joanne in the kitchen retrieving cups and tea bags and filling a kettle with water to boil. She relaxed and enjoyed the domestic scene that she'd played out in her mind many times in hopes it would one day become reality. She sank back on the couch and was surprised at how contented she felt. She certainly didn't miss Paul, but she'd just settled into her house making it her own. It seemed fate was in charge now, and as she watched Joanne approach with two cups of steaming tea, she felt happiness. "Thank you." She brushed her fingers over Joanne's as she accepted her cup.

"You're welcome." Joanne sat next to her with her thigh pressed against hers. "I'm glad you're here." She said in almost a whisper.

"I'm glad I'm here, too." She sipped her tea. "I've been thinking about my house."

"Do you want to go back?"

"I'm not sure. There's nothing there for me, and I want us to be together. I know that. And Mom is here."

"It sounds like you've been doing some heavy thinking."

"This is a big decision." Shanna smiled. "A life changing one."

"Relax, baby. You don't need to make it right this minute. We'll help the neighbors with the hurricane damage and then you can decide."

Shanna pulled Joanne into her arms and kissed her. "You are very precious to me."

"And you are to me." Joanne cuddled closer to her.

Shanna's phone interrupted her intended exploration of Joanne's lips. "Hello, Mom." she hugged Joanne closer. "We'd love to. Thank you. We'll see you about six. Thank you." Shanna disconnected the call and turned to Joanne. "Mom's invited us to dinner tonight. I hope you don't mind that I accepted for both of us."

"Of course not. I'm looking forward to it." Joanne took her hand and tugged her to the bedroom.

Shanna settled next to Joanne on the bed. "This is a good idea," she said before beginning to trail kisses along her neck to her chest.

Joanne rolled away interrupting her exploration. "I need to talk to you."

"Okay." Shanna held her close. "What's up?"

"I feel like you're pushing me away. Maybe to protect me? I want you here with me. I want us to make a life together. Is that something you think you'd want?"

"Oh, Joanne. I'm sorry if you feel I'm pushing you away. That's not my intention. I'm finally living my true self and trying to get used to it. I've pretended to be a straight happy wife of an attorney for so many years I might need time to feel like myself. Mom knows that I've been pretending with Paul. She and I had a long talk a few years ago, and I told her I promised I'd keep trying with Paul. Dad never knew and I think he believed I was happy with him."

"I'm sorry you lost your dad before he got to know you. And I'm sorry you had to pretend with Paul."

Shanna took Joanne's hands in hers. "I got used to pretending with Paul that I was at least content, but when I felt the toll it was taking on me, I gave up. He was having an affair with one of the women in his office and hardly noticed that we had nothing left between us. It was a huge relief when we split up. All I know is that you are the one I choose to be with." She kissed her.

"And you are who I choose to be with." Joanne pulled her on top of her.

"I think this will work out just fine then." Shanna wrapped her arms around her and held her tight. "What time is dinner?"

"Six. We have plenty of time." She kissed her.

❖

"Hi, Betty. Thanks for inviting us." Joanne handed her a carton of ice cream when they arrived at her house.

"Thank you for bringing desert. June called me today to thank you again for helping her."

"I'm glad we were able to," Shanna said. "I hope we'll be able to help some of your other neighbors who need it."

"Do you have that neighborhood directory?" Joanne asked. "We want to check on everyone to see if they need any help."

"I do." She retrieved the booklet from a drawer and handed it to Joanne. "That's nice of you to help. I know many of the neighbors need it but can't afford to hire anyone."

"After we eat, we'll talk about our plan. You can be our bookkeeper. Help us keep track of who, what, and when. We probably could start a rebuilding fund. Anyone who's able to contribute can and if they can't, there would be something to borrow from."

"I think that's a fine idea." Betty beamed.

"I believe we've just made my mom's day," Shanna said as they walked back to Joanne's after dinner.

"She does seem quite excited by our plan." Joanne took Shanna's hand.

"I'll go shopping tomorrow for some work clothes. I only packed one suitcase when we rushed to get here. Will you help me?" Shanna asked.

"Absolutely."

CHAPTER TWENTY-SEVEN

"We're going to have our work cut out for us," Joanne said as she reviewed the number of neighbors requesting help with repairs.

"We'll do what we can." Shanna walked out of the bedroom wearing her new jeans and work shirt. "What do you think?" She lifted her arms and twirled.

"Sexy." Joanne pulled her into her arms and kissed her.

"I'm not supposed to look sexy. I'm supposed to look like I'm ready to get to work."

"Okay. That too."

"Let's get to it. Who's first on the list?"

"The Levine's have 'piles of stuff' in their driveway and can't get their car out. Let's take care of them first." Joanne grabbed a box of garbage bags and took Shanna's hand to lead her out the door. "Boy, they weren't kidding about piles of stuff." Joanne studied the driveway trying to decide where to start. "I think we're going to need a wagon of some kind. All this won't fit into garbage bags."

"We can move it out to the lawn so the driveway is clear at least," Shanna suggested.

Joanne put on her gloves and began the task of moving the debris. "I'll call the city and see if they have a plan for curbside pickup. We may not have to do more than make a neat pile."

"That would make our jobs a lot easier if we only had to drag things curbside." Shanna tossed a board onto the pile.

Joanne began to walk to the next house when Mr. Levine hurried toward them. "I just called the city. They told me all I had to do was make sure nothing spilled out onto the road and they'll be here to pick it up on Tuesday." He was breathless when he stopped talking.

"Great! You should be all set then." Joanne smiled as he grabbed her into a hug.

"Ready for the next one?" Shanna asked.

"Yes. This means we'll be able to get done faster." Joanne crossed the Levines off her list and started toward the next neighbor.

"I'm pooped," Shanna said as she sat on a neighbor's retainer wall. "How many more do we have?"

"Only one." Joanne sat next to her. "It's this house and it doesn't look too bad." She pointed to their driveway.

"Okay. Let's get this done." Shanna stood, took Joanne's hand, and pulled her up.

"We can just start moving things out of the driveway. Maybe they'll see us and come out." She dragged a large piece of their mangled carport out to the street and returned for more. Shanna helped her with the rest of it and finished by sweeping the driveway. "Still no one came out?" she asked.

"Not that I've seen," Shanna replied. "Let's knock on the door again." She knocked and rang the bell several times. "Maybe they're not home. Let's let the Levines know we're done." Joanne knocked on the Levines' door and got no answer.

"Their car is here." Joanne walked to the backyard and looked into a back window. "Shanna! Come quick." Joanne picked up a rock and smashed the window before crawling through it. She scrambled to remember the CPR training she took years ago. Mr. Levine lay on his back on the bed not moving. Not breathing. She began chest compressions and called out to Shanna. Twenty minutes later, the paramedics arrived and took over the resuscitation.

Shanna had Mrs. Levine seated on the porch when Joanne went outside. "Are they taking him to the hospital?"

"Yes. The paramedics say you saved his life." Mrs. Levine wrapped her arms around her and buried her face on her shoulder as she cried.

"He's in good hands," Joanne whispered. "They'll take good care of him."

"We're so careful with his diet and he walks every day just like his doctor recommends." She began crying harder.

"We can take you to the hospital," Shanna said.

"Thank you, dear, but our daughter will be here soon. She can take me."

"That's good. We'll wait for her with you." Joanne led her into the house and they sat on her couch. "Can I get you something?" she offered.

"No, thank you, dear. I'll be fine, but thank you both for your help. I wouldn't have known what to do except call 911."

Joanne opened the door when she heard Mrs. Levine's daughter arrive.

"Thank you for helping Mom. I'm grateful you could be here for her."

"No problem. We'll leave you to take her to the hospital. Be careful." Joanne hugged her before following Shanna out the door.

"Whew. I'm glad we could be there to help her, but I'm glad their daughter's here."

"Me too. I hope he's going to be okay."

"Ready to go home?"

"Oh yes." Joanne took Shanna's hand as they walked back to her house.

"Would you mind if we went to Mom's for a little while?"

"Not at all. We can tell her about Mr. Levine."

Joanne changed her clothes and waited for Shanna. She looked forward to seeing Betty and having a cup of tea with her.

"Ready?" Shanna kissed her lightly.

"Yep." Joanne took her hand as they walked across the street.

"This is a nice surprise," Betty said as she opened the door for them. "I was just about to settle in to watch TV."

"I'm hoping you're ready for a cup of tea." Joanne smiled.

"Always. Come on in." Betty put a kettle on the stove. "How did the cleanup go today?"

Joanne looked at Shanna waiting for her to speak.

"Mr. Levine went to the hospital today. Joanne gave him CPR, which probably saved his life."

"We don't know that for sure." Joanne said.

"Well, his wife said his doctor has warned him of a weak heart and possible heart attack."

"I know. Eileen has him on a strict diet and he's supposed to take daily walks." Betty wrung her hands together. "I hope he'll be okay."

"He probably will be, Mom. Let's sit and relax. Do you still have that bottle of wine?"

"I do, honey." Betty opened the wine bottle and filled two glasses. "Can I get you anything, Joanne?"

"A cup of tea sounds lovely. I can make it. You two relax." Joanne made a cup of tea for herself and settled next to Shanna who sipped her wine. She'd never resented or envied Stacy when she drank alcohol, but a sliver of discomfort made its way through her seated next to Shanna while she drank wine. She drank her tea and took a deep breath to relax. It had been a busy day, but she felt good that they were able to help their neighbor. She forced away sleepiness by concentrating on the conversation. Betty was updating them on her neighbor helping neighbor plan and Shanna told her about their plans for helping with the repairs. She shifted in her seat to fight off drowsiness.

"I'm pooped." Shanna stood and stretched before reaching for her hand. "Ready to head home?"

"I am. Thanks for the tea, Betty." She hugged her and followed Shanna out the door. "I like that you called this home." Joanne kissed her softly.

"It feels right being here with you. I'll need to decide about my house eventually, and go back to get the rest of my clothes, but I like being with you and near my mom."

"Let's get some rest tonight and decide in the morning about the next neighbor to help."

"Sounds good to me. I'm tired. That glass of wine made me sleepy, too."

Joanne held Shanna in her arms long after she'd fallen asleep. She reflected on how much her life had changed since she left Michigan. Other than Heather there was no one left there for her. Stacy had probably moved on to someone else, and the thought didn't bother her. She held Shanna as she slept and sighed with contentment. This was where she belonged. It seemed this was her destiny.

❖

Joanne woke to the warmth of Shanna's body spooning her from behind. She snuggled closer and whimpered at the feel of her hand cradling her breast. Her whimpers became moans when Shanna squeezed her nipple gently and circled it with her fingers. "Keep that up, baby, and we won't get out of bed today."

"Mm. I couldn't resist. You're so warm and soft and sexy." Shanna kissed her bare shoulder and nuzzled her neck as she skimmed her hand down her belly. "I want to make you come." She pulled her closer and slid her fingers into her heat.

Joanne squirmed and arched into Shanna's touch. "You're definitely getting your wish." She covered Shanna's hands with hers and surged into orgasm. Joanne woke half an hour later to an empty bed. She rose and put on her robe before heading to the kitchen. She smiled at the scene. Betty sat at her table eating scrambled eggs, and Shanna stood at the stove cooking more eggs.

"You're just in time." Shanna grinned.

Besides being glad she'd put on her robe, she was happy to see Betty looking relaxed in her kitchen. "Sounds good to me."

"I couldn't find your toaster, though."

"That's because I don't have one. I'll have to get one the next time I'm at the store."

CHAPTER TWENTY-EIGHT

Shanna dished the scrambled eggs from the pan onto Joanne's plate.

"Thanks for cooking. I'm glad you're here this morning, Betty. Did you find the orange juice, babe?"

"I haven't looked."

Joanne retrieved the juice from the refrigerator and poured herself and Shanna a glass. "Betty?"

"Yes, please." She held up her empty glass to be filled. "Thank you."

"Have you heard how Mr. Levine is doing?"

"No. I thought I'd call Eileen today. He'll be in the hospital for at least two days."

"Is that a long time for a heart attack?"

"I don't think so. If it's a bad one, I'd expect longer. I guess I don't know for sure." Betty looked frustrated.

Shanna sat next to Betty. "It's all right. We'll go talk to Eileen and she'll know if he's up for visitors." She took a forkful of eggs and swallowed.

"Are you two going to continue helping neighbors today?" Betty sat back in her chair and drank her coffee.

"We are. We'll check on Mrs. Levine first."

"I think there's only a few left that need their driveways cleared. The first thing we did was make sure people could get out of their house in an emergency."

"I'm proud of you two." Betty stood and hugged them.

"Thanks, Mom, I'll bet there are many folks here that would do the same thing if they could." Shanna took a bite of food and swallowed.

"We decided we're the young ones around here, so we took on the task." Joanne grinned.

"I thank you from all of them." Betty smiled. "I'm taking this 'older one' home."

Shanna hugged her mother. "We'll bring over your chicken if the store has any." She sat with Joanne to finish her coffee. "We made Mom happy this morning. She was nervous about us."

"You mean like us as a couple? She seems to approve. I got the impression she was happy we found each other. Am I wrong?"

"No. You're not wrong. She wants to see us happy, but worries that others may not."

"Huh. Are you comfortable here with me?"

"Oh, honey, yes." Shanna stood and pulled Joanne into her arms. "I don't care what anyone else thinks or says. I care about you. About us as a couple."

"Good, because I think of us as a couple, too. I've never been so happy." Joanne kissed her.

"Shall we take a shower before going to the store?" Shanna grinned and pulled Joanne toward the bathroom.

She locked the bathroom door and pulled her clothes off. She reached for Joanne's and stepped into the shower when they were both naked. She adjusted the water temperature and pulled Joanne against her under the spray of water. She squirted body wash on her hands and began smoothing it over Joanne's shoulders and to her breasts before spreading it over her own breasts and pulling Joanne against her. She moaned when Joanne swayed rubbing their nipples against each other and sliding her palm down her belly. She stopped when her fingers reached her clit and she circled it with her finger. She alternated between pressing against it and circling it until Shanna pushed against her and shuddered. Her legs felt like rubber and Joanne pulled her tightly against her, holding her up.

"I've got you, baby," Joanne whispered.

"Well, that didn't work quite like I planned it."

"It was perfect." Joanne leaned her head back and took a deep breath. "At this rate, we won't get much done today."

"We will." Shanna took her hand and pulled her to the bedroom. "No touching. We'll get dressed and get to the store. Maybe we can get mom's chicken anyway." She dressed and went to the kitchen to make a list.

"Ready?" Joanne asked.

"I am. Let's get this done." Shanna took her hand and led her to the car. "Hopefully, the store won't be too busy."

Joanne pushed the cart and Shanna picked out the chickens and the other items. "It looks like we're done."

"I think so, too," Shanna said. She loaded everything into the car and Joanne drove them home. "I'll take the chickens to Mom and be back soon." She kissed Joanne and went across the street before she started something again. "It's me, Mom. I have your chicken," she called out from the door.

"Thank you, dear. Come in." Her mother met her at the door. "Was the store busy?"

"No. It went quickly."

"Would you like some wine or a cup of tea?"

Shanna wanted to get back to finish what she and Joanne had started. "Not tonight, but thanks, Mom."

"Okay, thank you, again."

Shanna forced herself to walk back across the street instead of running. "I'm back," she called out from the kitchen.

"I'm back here," Joanne called from the bedroom.

Shanna went to look for her and found her stretched out on the bed completely naked.

"I'm glad you're home. How's Betty?"

"She's fine." Shanna pulled off her clothes as she spoke. She crawled onto the bed and gathered Joanne in her arms.

"Hmm. I hoped you wouldn't stay too long. I was missing you." Joanne rolled over on top of Shanna and slid her thigh between her legs.

Shanna bucked underneath her and pulled her against herself as she came. "Wow. I've been thinking about you since this morning."

"Me too. Rest now, baby." She wrapped her arms around Shanna and sighed before drifting into sleep.

❖

Shanna woke before dawn and enjoyed the quiet peacefulness of the morning. Joanne lay sleeping soundly next to her, and she gently slipped her arm over her and cuddled against her. Lying in bed holding Joanne was the most serene feeling she could imagine. Why she ever thought she would be content with Paul made no sense to her now. Joanne was soft and gentle. She fell back asleep enveloped in her warmth.

"Time to rise and shine," a soft voice drifted into her awareness. "I have an exciting bowl of oatmeal waiting for you."

Soft kisses followed the voice and Shanna snuggled into Joanne's arms. "Oatmeal?"

"With cinnamon and warm milk." Joanne pulled her closer and nuzzled her neck. "I'll add raisins if you like."

Shanna rolled on top of Joanne and kissed her. "I'd like a drizzle of honey, too."

"Yes, your highness. It'll be waiting for you at your throne." Joanne kissed her and rolled her off so she stood next to the bed.

"I guess it's time to get up." Shanna put on her robe and followed Joanne to the kitchen. "Wow. This is nice." The kitchen table was set with two bowls of oatmeal, spoons, forks, and coffee. Two candles burned in the center.

"Does your highness require orange juice?"

"Not this morning, thank you." Shanna caressed her neck and ran her fingers down her chest between her breasts. "I think I require you, though." She brushed her hands over her breasts and was pleased when her nipples hardened under her caress.

"My masterpieces will get cold. Can you hold on until we've eaten?"

"I suppose." She sighed dramatically and sat at the table. She ate a spoonful of the oatmeal and hummed. "This is good, sweetheart." She continued to eat until the bowl was empty.

"Thank you." Joanne sat across from her and smiled before she picked up her spoon and ate. "It's important to get just the right balance of cinnamon to milk." She sipped her coffee.

"We have a busy day ahead. I thought we could start with the Levine's. Check on her and get an update on his condition."

Shanna nodded. "I'm not sure how long he'll be in the hospital, but it would be nice for him to come home to a fixed window. We can put clear plastic over it anyway."

"Yeah. I'm not sure I'm able to replace a window." Joanne frowned. "I'll look at it though."

"Thanks for making the delicious oatmeal." Shanna picked up their empty bowls and cups and washed them in the sink before wrapping her arms around Joanne and kissing her. "I don't suppose we have time for more than kisses, do we?"

"We will later." Joanne pulled her into her arms and kissed her. "Do you want to check on your mom before you go? I'll meet you at the Levines'."

"Yeah. I suppose being right across the street now means I can check on her easily. I used to call her every other day."

"Give her my best. I'll see you later, sweetheart." Joanne kissed her and went to collect supplies.

"Be careful," Shanna said before walking across the street. "Hello, Mom," she called from the doorway.

"Hi, honey. Come on in. This is a nice surprise. I just made a fresh pot of coffee." She poured two cups and handed one to Shanna when she entered the house. "Shall we sit outside? It's a beautiful day. I guess this is the calm after the storm."

"Sounds good." Shanna sat next to her mother in one of her lawn chairs.

"Is Joanne coming over?"

"Probably later. She went to try to fix the Levines' broken window."

"He's still in the hospital. Eileen was beside herself yesterday when I went to see her."

"Well, I hope we can fix her window for her at least." Shanna sipped the coffee her mother handed her.

"I'd be willing to donate to help if they need it. I have the name and number for the company doing work in the neighborhood. Hopefully, they're not overcharging for their work."

"I'll walk down there and see how things are going after I finish my coffee." She considered telling her mother about Joanne's special oatmeal this morning, but changed her mind. It was their private experience. The special part belonged to her.

CHAPTER-TWENTY-NINE

"M rs. Levine?" Joanne called to her from the front porch. "Joanne. Good morning. Please call me Eileen." She opened the door and led her to the dining room. "I just made fresh coffee. Please sit." She pointed to a chair.

Joanne smiled. "Thank you," she said when Eileen placed a cup in front of her. "So, I have an idea for a temporary fix for your broken window."

"Oh, thank you, dear." Eileen sat across from her and drank her coffee.

"I have some heavy plastic that I can secure to the frame. That will keep the heat out and any rain. There's a company in the area that's doing some of the heavy repairs. I'm sure they can replace the window if you want them to."

Eileen set her cup down and frowned. "I've heard about them. Claudia next door has hired them to replace her carport. I'm not sure we can afford to pay them." She rested her hand on Joanne's. "I'm sorry I can't pay you much either." She had tears in her eyes.

"Eileen." Joanne stood and pulled Eileen into a hug. "I'm your neighbor and your friend, I hope. I absolutely don't expect you to pay me anything. I'm able to help and I want to. I have no doubt that if I needed something you'd offer to help."

"Of course I would." Eileen wiped her eyes with a napkin.

"I'm going to go home and get my hammer and staple gun. It shouldn't take me long."

"Oh, honey. Check in our shed first. My husband used to be very handy. He's got who knows what collected in there."

"I will. Thank you." Joanne found the shed door unlocked and went in search of supplies. Eileen wasn't kidding about who knew what was in that shed. Not only was the shed full, it was meticulously organized. He had several hammers hanging from pegboard above a wooden bench. She opened the many drawers in a cabinet against a side wall and found a staple gun and heavy-duty staples. She grabbed a measuring tape from another drawer and went to the back of the house to measure the broken window frame. She collected the necessary plastic and wood for a temporary frame and it didn't take her long to replace the broken window with her plastic covered one. She returned the tools and took a last look at the amazing shed before locking the door and heading back to the house. "You should be set for a while," she told Eileen.

Joanne cringed at Eileen's tears. "It'll be okay." She tentatively reached for her and Eileen slipped into her arms and cried harder. She wrapped her arms around her and waited until her sobs subsided. "Mr. Levine will be home soon and the bedroom window is covered enough so no rain will get in."

"Thank you!" She collected herself and stroked Joanne's cheek gently.

Joanne took note of the houses as she walked home. Most had lost carports and a few had workers measuring while talking to the homeowners. She'd call them later and make an appointment to have Eileen's window replaced and get an estimate on replacing her carport. She settled on her couch with a cup of coffee and turned on the television when she got home. She watched the news coverage of the cleanup for a while before taking a shower and heading across the street to Betty's.

"How'd it go, honey?" Shanna took her hand and squeezed.

"All done. I'll call that company to replace her window, but it's covered now. Any word on Mr. Levine?"

"I talked to Eileen last night and she wasn't sure when he'd be home, but it sounds like he will be. I take that as good news." Betty smiled.

"Yes. That's good. She's worried. I wasn't sure she was going to let me leave after I finished the window."

"She's scared and lonely. I've invited her to dinner tonight, and I hope she comes." Betty sighed.

Joanne looked at her watch. "I'm going to work for a few hours today, so I better go change."

"I'll walk with you." Shanna stood. "Thanks for the coffee and company this morning, Mom."

"Anytime, you two."

"I didn't know you had to work today. I'd have kept you in bed longer." Shanna kissed her quickly.

"I got a voice mail message from my boss while I was at the Levines'. They're short-handed due to the mess everyone has to clean up. He was thrilled to find me available. It'll only be for a few hours. I should be home by four thirty." Joanne held Shanna's hand as they walked.

"I'll plan to get some work done while you're gone. It'll work out well." Shanna squeezed her hand.

"I gave you the password for my Internet, didn't I?"

"Yep. I'm all set."

Joanne changed into her work clothes when she got home and packed a lunch. "I'll see you later, honey." She kissed Shanna.

"Wow. You clean up pretty well. You look damn sexy. I may have to hang out at this bank to keep an eye on you."

"Sweetheart, you are the only one I'm interested in. I was told by the bank when I applied there that they expected me to be dressed 'professionally.' I guess this meets their approval because my boss has never complained."

"Well, I certainly approve. You look professional and very sexy." Shanna kissed her.

"I'll see you later." She made herself a peanut butter sandwich, kissed Shanna, and went to work.

❖

"Thanks for coming in, Joanne," her boss said.

"No problem. I just finished helping a neighbor and didn't plan anything except dinner tonight. I imagine there've been people coming in to get cash."

"Yes. The power has been out in several areas and credit card readers don't work. So, thanks again for coming in."

Joanne worked until the last person left and signed out for the day. "I'll see you Monday," she said as she locked down her station and left.

❖

"I'm home," she said from the doorway. She grabbed a bottle of water and went to the living room. Shanna wasn't there so she went to what she now considered as their bedroom. She found her sound asleep on the bed. She quietly undressed and slid under the covers with her. She sighed when Shanna snuggled into her while still asleep. She drifted off and enjoyed the heat of Shanna's body in her arms.

"I'm glad you're back," Shanna murmured. "I missed you."

Joanne kissed her and nuzzled her neck. "My boss was very glad to see me. I was the only teller who came in and there was a line of people hoping to access their accounts to get cash."

"Ah. The power is still out in many areas. They can't use the credit card readers." Shanna squirmed closer.

"Right. I'm glad I could help him out. The bank's running on generator power, but the automatic tellers aren't reliable. Sometimes they work and sometimes not. It'll give me a paycheck this week, too."

"That reminds me that I want to talk about that. Finances I mean." Shanna sat up but kept a hand on her shoulder. "If I'm going to live here, I need to help with expenses. I just finished editing one of the manuals I had, and I'll get paid in a couple of days. What would you think about a joint bank account?"

"I like the idea. What about your house?"

"I've been thinking about that, too. Can you take a few days off work? If we fly back to South Carolina, I'll put the house on the market and we can drive back in my car."

"I think that would work. We'll plan it, and I'll talk to my boss when we have the details finalized." Joanne took a deep breath. "Are you sure that's what you want? You've only been here a short time."

"I'm sure, Joanne, but we can't make a decision like this unless we're both sure. I'm not opposed to giving us more time, if you need it."

Joanne pulled her into her arms. Did she?

CHAPTER THIRTY

"A re you sure you don't mind going with me, honey?"
Shanna smiled at her mother's uncertainty. "Of course
I don't, Mom. I'm sure Eileen is anxious to get her husband home.
I'll drive and you sit in the back seat with her."

"Thank you. She's so nervous, I know it would be hard for her
to drive. Is Joanne back to work now?"

"She is." Shanna considered talking to her mother about her
permanent move to Florida, but decided she'd wait until they were
back from the hospital.

"I'm glad. I know she was worried about it."

"Yes, she was. Things seem to be settling down now. People
are back to work and recovering from the damages."

"They are. Our neighborhood watch group is back to meeting
weekly again."

"That's great, Mom."

"Are you planning to stay longer, honey?"

"I hope so. Joanne and I are working that out now. I was going
to tell you about it later."

"I'd never presume to tell you what to do. You and Joanne are
adults and whatever you two decide is your business. I'll just say
that I'm glad you found each other. You both seem happy."

"We are. I've never felt this way about anyone before.
We care about each other and we've settled into a comfortable

relationship." She pulled into the hospital parking lot and turned off the car. "Here we are."

Shanna watched as the hospital personnel helped Mr. Levine into the back seat of the car. He looked rested and wore a huge smile. He was probably happy to be alive and going home.

"Ready?" she waited for an answer from the back seat.

"Yes," her mother said.

She drove carefully aware of her precious cargo. "We're home." She parked in the driveway and got out to help Mr. Levine out of the car.

"Thank you, honey." Eileen hugged her.

She followed close behind them as they entered the house. He looked to be weak, but he was able to walk and had no trouble with the one step into the house. She made sure he was settled comfortably in a chair at the dining room table before leaving with her mother.

"Thank you, again, honey. I'm so glad he's doing well. He looked happy to be home, didn't he?"

"He did. I suppose I would be, too, if I just recovered from a heart attack. He had to be scared."

"Eileen sure was. They've been married sixty years. She'd be devastated to lose him."

Shanna considered what it would be like to be with someone sixty years. She calculated in her head and realized she and Joanne probably wouldn't have that long, but maybe they'd make forty. "They must have married young."

"She told me they began dating when they were sixteen and married at eighteen. Her parents weren't too happy, but grew to love him almost as much as she did."

"What a nice love story. I'm glad he survived this heart attack, and I hope they have many more years together."

"Me too, honey."

Shanna cringed. Her mother must be thinking about Shanna's father. Taken way too soon. She wrapped her arm around her. "Ready to go home?"

"Yes." She said good-bye to her friends, and Shanna took her home.

"Would you like to come in for a cup of tea?"

"Thanks, Mom, but I have a new manual I need to get started on."

"Okay. I'll talk to you tomorrow. Say hello to Joanne."

"I will." Shanna went across the street and settled on the couch with her laptop. She worked for an hour and backed up her work before starting dinner. Joanne would be home soon and she liked to have dinner almost ready so they could eat together. They'd settled into a comfortable routine, but hadn't talked more about making their situation permanent. She needed to make a decision about her house. There didn't seem much sense in continuing to pay utilities and insurance on it if it remained empty, but she had no desire to leave Joanne and move back. She missed her car, too. She mixed the ingredients for chili and set the stove to simmer before going back to the couch to wait for Joanne.

"I'm home," Joanne said.

"Hey, honey." Shanna kissed her.

"How did it go with Mr. Levine?" Joanne sat next to her and rested her arm around her.

"We got him home and into his house. Eileen was grateful."

"Good. I hoped he was recovered enough to go home."

"Did you know they've been married for sixty years?"

"Wow. No I didn't. That's amazing."

Joanne was quiet for so long Shanna worried. "You okay?"

"Oh yes. I was just figuring. I almost said I hope we have sixty years together, but we'll shoot for at least forty, okay?"

"I think that's a very good number." Shanna pushed her onto the couch and lay on top of her. "A very good number." She kissed her until they were both breathless.

"I talked to my boss today," Joanne said between kisses. "He told me just to let him know when I'll be gone."

"Yeah? Are you going somewhere?" Shanna nuzzled her neck.

"I thought maybe we would."

"Where are we going?"

"We talked about going back to your house to do something with it. I thought maybe we could fly there and do whatever you're going to do with it, and drive your car back. Would that work for you?"

"Yes. I like that idea." She pulled Joanne on top of her and kissed her. "I was a little worried you'd forgotten about it."

"I'm sorry you were worried. I don't ever want you to worry." Joanne sat up and wrapped her arms around her.

"I'm afraid we're human. I think worry is a part of being in that condition."

"Shall we pick a date to leave and make plans?"

"Can we do it tomorrow?" Shanna pushed her down on the couch and lay on top of her before kissing her. "I think we'll be busy tonight."

Shanna rolled over and sighed as she felt the heat of Joanne's body next to her that night. Her mind raced with plans. Her mother could probably take them to the airport. Would all her clothes fit in the trunk of her car? She'd need to talk to a Realtor and see if she could sell the house furnished. Would her drafting table fit in her car? Maybe she should rent a U-Haul.

"Sweetheart?" Joanne murmured.

"Sorry, baby. Am I keeping you up?"

"I'd hoped I put you to sleep earlier. Do I need to try again?" Joanne rolled on top of her and kissed her.

"I can't seem to shut off my mind."

"It's okay. Make a list tomorrow. Write everything down that's keeping you awake. Then you can let it go."

"I will." She took Joanne's hand and placed it between her legs. "Touch me?"

"Oh yes." Joanne stroked her wetness and massaged her clit with slippery fingers. She pulled her close and circled her nipple with her tongue.

Shanna keened and arched into her touch until she tumbled into orgasm. "Oh my." She rolled to her side and kissed Joanne's breast before falling into a dreamless sleep.

Shanna woke the next morning to the scent of coffee. She opened her eyes and smiled. Joanne sat on the side of the bed holding two cups of the steaming brew. "Coffee in bed. You're spoiling me." She sipped her coffee and enjoyed the feeling of being cared about. "You're quite a catch, you know. How is it no one has stolen your heart before me?"

Joanne stared at her for a few seconds before looking down. "I told you about my fetal alcohol syndrome disorder. It causes gaps in my memory sometimes. I've had therapy since I was sixteen and will probably need it forever, and all that can be hard on relationships. I think that's why Stacy and I were never close. It takes patience." Joanne shrugged.

"Well, I want to be very close." Shanna set her coffee cup aside and pulled Joanne on top of her. "And I have lots of patience." Joanne was a grown woman with a condition that affected her whole life but for which she wasn't responsible. An intense sense of protectiveness overtook Shanna as she held Joanne as she dozed in her arms. She closed her eyes and enjoyed the heat of their bodies mingling. She woke to Joanne nuzzling her neck. "Mm. Is it time to get up?"

"Probably. We have a trip to plan."

Shanna finished working on the final manual on her pile and breathed a sigh of relief. She was free to concentrate on her trip back to South Carolina.

"I've got lunch ready," Joanne said.

"Thanks for making it." Shanna took a bite of her sandwich and swallowed before speaking. "I checked on a few flights this morning. There's one leaving at nine a.m. next Saturday. Would that be okay for you?"

"I don't work on Saturdays, so it should be fine."

"Sounds good. I'll see you tonight." Joanne kissed her and went to work.

Shanna drank a cup of coffee as she started a reminder list for the trip. She wrote down what she wanted to bring back from her house and what she could leave behind before she called the Realtor.

"Hello, *House Sales.*" The Realtor sounded nice enough.

"Hello. My name is Shanna Mills and I have a house I need to sell." Shanna gave her the address and details. "I plan to be there next week, but there's a spare key under the flowerpot next to the garage." She disconnected the call and continued her list.

CHAPTER THIRTY-ONE

Thank you, Dave. It shouldn't take more than a couple days. I'll let you know the exact date." Joanne thanked her boss, finished her work day, and went home. Shanna was at the kitchen table working so Joanne kissed her quickly and went to the bedroom to make a call.

"Hi, Joanne. Everything okay?" Heather asked.

"It is. I haven't talked to you in a while."

"Has something come up, Joanne?"

"I met someone and she's become very special to me. We plan to live together."

"Am I right to assume you told her about your FASD?"

"I did and she's supportive. I'd love for you to meet her."

"I have a few days off. How about if I come on Wednesday?"

"We're planning to leave Saturday for South Carolina to get Shanna's stuff. Could you come the following weekend?"

"Sure. Let's plan for Saturday next week."

"That would be great. I'll let Shanna know you're coming."

"Okay. I'll only plan to stay a couple of days. It will be great to see you and meet Shanna."

"I'll see you next Saturday."

Joanne disconnected the call and went to tell Shanna. "I have good news. Heather's coming for a visit."

"She's your friend and therapist isn't she?"

"Yes. She'll be here next Saturday and stay a couple of days."

"Great! We'll plan a couple of nice meals."

"I told my boss I'd be gone a few days when we go to get your stuff and let him know when."

"Great. Let's get the flight reserved today for Saturday morning. We should be able to be home by Tuesday."

"I'm looking forward to introducing you to Heather."

"And I'm looking forward to meeting her."

"She's the reason I'm able to function as well as I do. I'm not sure where I'd be without her. How does pizza sound for dinner tonight?"

"Sounds good. Want me to order it?"

"Nope." Joanne went to the freezer and pulled out a large frozen pizza. "I'll put it in the oven."

"Okay. Shall we watch TV while we eat?"

"Sure." Joanne put napkins and silverware on the coffee table and turned on the TV.

"This is nice." Shanna cuddled next to her.

"It is." Joanne pulled her closer.

Joanne relaxed and enjoyed the heat from Shanna's body next to her. "Are you happy here, Shanna?"

"I am. Why do you ask?"

"We're about to move all your belongings here. I'm very happy about that."

Shanna grinned. "I'm very very happy about it."

"I'm going to give your mom a copy of my key. Just in case, while we're gone."

"Good idea." Shanna was quiet for a while. "I'm going to sell my house furnished if I can. I don't want to pay to have beds, dressers, and living room furniture moved. We don't have room for it all here anyway. I need my drafting table and chair for my sketching though. I don't think I showed you that."

"No, you didn't. I see I have more to learn about you." Joanne kissed her. "I look forward to it. I'll be right back." Joanne went to the extra bedroom to check the condition. She stripped the bed and moved the few items in the closet to their bedroom before heading back to the couch. "I checked the room for Heather."

"Good idea." Shanna snuggled closer to her.

Joanne looked forward to spending time with Heather. Since her parents died and Stacy showed little interest in her, Heather was her last connection to Michigan. She'd been raised in the state so different from Florida, but decided to make this her home. The hurricane had brought her Shanna and a neighborhood of potential friends. Her life seemed filled with possibilities she never could have imagined when her parents had sat her down and explained her condition and its limitations to her. Heather had supported and guided her through graduation from high school and a year of community college and she hoped she'd be proud of her now. She pushed aside her musings to concentrate on their upcoming trip.

"You all right, honey?" Shanna asked.

"I am. I was just thinking about Heather and how much influence she's had on my life. I'm able to do so much because of her."

"I look forward to meeting her." Shanna squeezed her hand.

Joanne kissed Shanna quickly and rose from the couch. "Do you have anything you need washed? I'm going to do a load of laundry."

"No, but thanks. I'm all set."

Joanne collected the clothes she planned to wash and put them into the washer. She realized she was obsessing but didn't care. Heather wouldn't be there until after they returned from Shanna's, but she wanted to be ready. She wanted to make Heather proud of her. She had a job, a house, and a girlfriend. She was able to manage her life as a responsible adult, and she owed much of that to her parents' and Heather's guidance throughout the years. She settled back on the couch next to Shanna and rested her arm around her.

"Are you finished with all this activity?" Shanna grinned and leaned into her.

"Sorry. I'm a little nervous."

"I can see that. Why?"

"I don't know. Heather has been my support for years when my parents were alive and after. I want to show her how self-sufficient I am now."

"Honey. You are one of the most responsible people I know. You're honest, caring, and responsible. She'll be proud of you." Shanna kissed her. "I am, too."

"Are you ready?" Joanne asked Shanna a week later as they prepared for their trip.

"I am."

"Let's get on with our adventure. I'm glad your mom was able to take us to the airport. She settled in her seat on the plane remembering the first time she'd flown with Heather. That time she was headed to what had ended up being her new home. This time she was joining her lover to collect her belongings. She relaxed and enjoyed the flight.

❖

"Here we are." Shanna slid out of the taxi and waited for Joanne to join her. They took their luggage into the house and plopped onto the couch. "I'm pooped."

"Yeah. Me too. Shall we nap before we begin packing?"

"Sounds good." Shanna took her hand and led her to the bedroom where they fell onto the bed. Joanne closed her eyes and fell asleep. She woke half an hour later alone. She rose to look for Shanna and found her in the room she called her art room. Beautiful paintings and pencil sketches lined the walls. A window shed afternoon sunlight into the room. "Nice room."

"It is. I love it. We'll make a nice room for you at home." Joanne hugged her.

"I think I have all the important things out. Will you help me load the car?"

"Of course. Let's do it." Joanne struggled with spatial issues at times so she relied on Shanna to direct fitting things into the car. She made sure Shanna had all the items important to her and closed the trunk. "It looks like the drafting table will have to slide in the back seat."

"Yeah. I think we can still fit our suitcases behind it on the seat." Shanna kissed her. "Thank you for your help. And for doing this."

"You're important to me, Shanna. I want you to be happy."

"McDonald's okay for dinner?" Shanna grabbed her car keys.

Joanne retrieved plates and set Shanna's kitchen table with the bag of fish sandwiches in the middle. "This was a good idea. We can stop there for breakfast tomorrow on the way home."

"The Realtor will be here at eight with the listing paperwork. We can leave right after that."

"Okay. Let me know what you need me to do to help." Joanne looked around feeling useless.

"I think we're done. If you see something you think we need just grab it."

Joanne grinned and grabbed Shanna around the waist and pulled her against her. "I got all I need." She kissed her.

Joanne wiped the table and took the garbage out to the end of the driveway the next morning to be picked up. She pulled the car out of the garage and waited for Shanna. Shanna had indicated the papers were signed and they were ready to leave so she put the address in the GPS and waited.

"Okay. Whew. I'm glad that's over. The Realtor had a pile of papers to sign, but it's done. Let's go home." Shanna kissed her and plopped into her seat.

Joanne pulled out of the driveway and headed for the expressway. "Ready for lunch?" she asked as she pulled into a Burger King parking lot an hour into their trip.

"Yes!" Shanna kissed her quickly before getting out of the car. "I'll drive now," Shanna said after they finished eating.

Joanne sat quietly and watched the scenery whiz by. She dozed off for a few minutes and startled awake when she felt the car stop.

"We need gas." Shanna smiled. "Didn't mean to wake you." She filled the tank and they started back on the road.

"I'm sorry I conked out on you," Joanne said softly.

"No problem. It shouldn't be too much longer now."

"Let me know if you need me to drive." Joanne fell asleep again.

"We're home," Shanna said and gently rested her hand on Joanne's arm.

Joanne woke and blinked. "Sorry again." She climbed out of the car and stretched. "Thanks for getting us here."

Shanna stretched when she got out of the car, too. "Whew. I'm glad that drive is over."

"Let's rest and eat before we unload the car." Joanne took Shanna's hand and led her to into the house.

CHAPTER THIRTY-TWO

B oy, I'm tired." Shanna plopped onto the bed and closed her eyes.

"Me too." Joanne cuddled next to her.

"I'll get the food we brought out of the car." Shanna slowly climbed out of bed and retrieved the bag with food in it and tossed it into the refrigerator before going back to bed.

"I'm so glad we didn't try to do that roundtrip in one day." Joanne pulled her into her arms.

"Yeah. It feels good to have it done. I was worried about it."

"I'm glad you can relax now." Joanne kissed her.

"Is it all right if I put my drafting table in the corner of the extra bedroom?"

"Sure. Wherever you want it."

Shanna drifted in and out of sleep for an hour and decided to get up and start unloading the car. She pulled her drafting table out first and put it in the extra bedroom facing the window. There wasn't a dogwood tree outside, but she could see the clouds and the tops of a few palm trees. She put a sheet of paper on her table and began to sketch a few palm trees swaying in the breeze. She sighed as she relaxed into her work. She hadn't realized how much she missed it. The finished product calmed her along with the knowledge her life was on a different track. One of her own choosing. When her house sold she'd have money to put into a saving account. She didn't know where her relationship with Joanne was going, but she needed to feel she could contribute to them as a couple.

"Want to see my first project here?" she asked when Joanne entered the room.

"Absolutely."

Shanna led her to her drafting table and held up her latest sketch.

"Very nice. You're pretty talented. Have you ever thought of selling your work?"

"No. That would make it feel like work. I draw because it relaxes me. I enjoy it as a hobby."

"I'm glad you found a place to do that. I've only used this room for storage. I like the idea of it being your studio."

Shanna rested her arms on her shoulders and pressed against her before kissing her. "I like being here with you. Thank you for traveling back with me to get my stuff."

"You're welcome. I'm happy that you wanted to move to be with me. I'm heating up chicken soup and have ham and cheese for sandwiches."

"Sounds good." Shanna hadn't realized how hungry she was.

"Hello?" Betty called from the doorway.

"Come on in," Joanne said. "Do you want to join us for lunch?"

"I just ate, but thank you." She came into the house and sat at the kitchen table. "How was your trip?"

"It went smoothly. I'm glad it's over." Shanna sighed.

"You two come over for dinner tonight. I want to hear all the details." Betty kissed her cheek and left.

"I guess we don't need to cook tonight." Joanne pulled Shanna into her arms. "I'm glad it's over, too."

"I feel a little off." Shanna pushed closer to Joanne. "It's a weird feeling. Almost like I'm lost."

"You're not lost, baby. You're here with me and we're going to finish lunch first and then I'll help you unload the car and get you settled in."

"I think I need you." She kissed Joanne. "I need you now." She took her hand and led her to the bedroom. Shanna pushed her onto the bed and lay on top of her. "Yes. I need to feel you everywhere." Shanna dozed after their lovemaking and pulled Joanne back when she tried to get up.

"It's okay, sweetheart. I'm not going anywhere." Joanne gathered her in her arms.

"I'm sorry. My life has changed so much it might take me a while to adjust."

"Changed for the better, love?" Joanne kissed her.

"Yes, for the better. I lived in that house for over seven years. I was fulfilling my parents' dream, not mine. They expected me to marry a man and have his children. After my father died, we both grieved and she stayed with me for a couple of weeks while we healed.

"I'm glad you were there for each other, and I hope to win her trust. I never want to hurt you or see you hurt." Joanne kissed her and held her close.

"Let's unload the car. I have my clothes to put away and my kitchen stuff."

"Okay. Let's get to it."

Shanna added her silverware to Joanne's in the kitchen drawers and sorted her plates and glassware. Most of it was old donations from her mother and valuable to her. She put her favorite coffee cup next to Joanne's in the cupboard and left the rest in a box for Good Will. She hung her clothes in Joanne's closet and sat on the bed to stare at it. Her stuff looked right here. She added her sheets to the drawer with Joanne's and her towels in the bathroom closet. She reviewed everything and relaxed. She and Joanne fit together well.

"I'm glad you're here." Joanne hugged her.

"I feel better now that I have my things put away. It's a strange feeling to go back to seeing my life as I lived it even though it wasn't what I wanted, and now seeing me here where I want to be with you and my stuff here, too."

"I think I understand what you mean. It's a life change for you."

"Not really a change, but sort of. I think it's recognition of what I want in life. Who I am. I've tried to live up to my parents' expectations for years and ignored the small voice urging me to make a change. To choose the life I wanted."

"I'm glad I'm the one you chose." Joanne took her hand and kissed her palm. "Shall we change and go to your mom's for dinner?"

Shanna checked her watch. "Yeah." She went to the bedroom and opened the closet as if she'd done it forever. She changed into nice slacks and a matching blouse.

"You look great." Joanne kissed her and went to change.

Shanna checked the cupboard and found a bottle of sparkling juice to take to her mother's. She smiled at the thought she and Joanne were going to her mother's for dinner as a couple.

"Ready?" Joanne asked as she wrapped her arms around her from behind and nuzzled her neck.

"Yep." She held up the bottle. "I think she likes this kind."

"Hi, Betty. Thanks for inviting us." Joanne hugged her when they entered the house.

"I'm thrilled to have you both here. You two must be tired. I know what a long drive that was, remember? Sit and we'll eat soon."

"I brought this for you." Shanna handed her mother the bottle of sparkling juice.

"Thank you, honey." She kissed her cheek. "Let's have a glass before dinner."

"You're spoiling us with all these offers of meals. It's wonderful though."

Shanna held Joanne's hand as they crossed the street to go home after dinner. "Mom seemed happy to have us for dinner. I worry she's lonely."

"We'll make a point of visiting her often and having her over for dinner." Joanne squeezed her hand. "She seemed happy to see us tonight."

"She was. Now that I'm all moved in, I'll spend some time with her daily. I think she'll like that."

Joanne pulled Shanna into her arms and kissed her. "You're a good daughter. Let me know what I can do to help."

"I will. Mom seems to enjoy us visiting her together. I'll talk to her about a once-a-week dinner or something. Does that work for you?"

"Sure. Just let me know when and where." She pulled Shanna against her and kissed her. "It's bedtime, isn't it?"

Shanna woke the next morning and snuggled closer to Joanne's body heat. Her life had taken an unexpected but very welcomed turn. She'd married Paul believing it was the right thing to do to satisfy her parents. Being with Joanne, living with her, and moving to Florida had been her decision, and she enjoyed the feeling of contentment knowing she was in charge of her life. Her mother seemed to embrace her decision and accept Joanne as Shanna's special person. She dozed off satisfied with the results.

Shanna woke half an hour later in Joanne's arms. "Morning, honey."

"I love waking up with you in my arms." Joanne pulled her close.

"I look forward to it for a long time to come." She kissed Joanne and climbed out of bed. "I'm making omelets this morning. We need to use up the eggs and cheese I had in my refrigerator."

"Shall we invite Betty...your mom to help us?"

"Good idea. I'll call her."

"Thank you for inviting me," Betty said as she set the Bundt cake she'd brought on the table.

"Thank you for bringing the cake." Joanne grinned and sliced three pieces.

"Have you heard from any more neighbors who need help?"

"I have, honey. I have a list at home for you."

Shanna looked at Joanne and received a nod and a wink. "Good. We'll check it out later today."

CHAPTER THIRTY-THREE

That would be great, Heather. I'm looking forward to seeing you and introducing you to Shanna," Joanne said to Heather on her phone. "Let me know when you finalize details."

Joanne disconnected the call and found Shanna working at her drafting table. She gently stroked her back before speaking. "I just talked to Heather. She's postponing her visit until next month."

"That's great, honey. We'll get this room ready for her." Shanna kissed her.

"I was thinking about a twin bed or a daybed. What do you think?"

"Is Heather married?"

"Yes, and she has a daughter, but I don't think she'd come with her. She's a junior at MSU."

"Maybe a double bed would be better."

"You're right. We'll get one. I'll see you later." Joanne kissed her and left for work. Joanne struggled to keep her mind on her tasks throughout the day. Heather had been her go-to person when her FASD had her confused and uncertain. Sessions with her had convinced her she could make her way in the world. Heather believed in her and gave her the confidence to believe in herself and she missed her. She finished her workday and went home. "Something smells good in here." She kissed Shanna who was standing at the stove.

"I made chili." Shanna covered the pot, turned, and pulled her into her arms.

"I like coming home to you." Joanne kissed her.

"I like you coming home to me. We can eat whenever you're ready."

"Any word on your house selling?" Joanne said between spoonfuls of chili.

"Not yet, but the Realtor left me a message that she's shown it several times. I have my fingers crossed."

"It's a nice house. I'm sure it'll go quickly."

"I hope so."

"I'll do the dishes and then I'd like to relax with you and a couple of pieces of Bundt cake."

"Sounds good to me," Shanna said.

"Shall we watch a movie tonight? I have *The Wizard of Oz* or *The Sound of Music.*"

"Either one is okay with me."

Joanne started the movie and settled next to Shanna on the couch to eat dessert.

"Damn." Shanna muttered as she looked at her phone.

"What is it, babe?" Joanne cringed at how upset Shanna looked.

"I just got a text from Paul! He's pissed because I put the house for sale."

"It's none of his business now is it?"

"No. I took his name off the deed when we divorced. He has no claim to it." Shanna stood.

"Sit, honey. He'll find out soon enough if he tries to block the sale."

"True. Damn him. I thought he was out of my life for good."

"He is. You're here with me and here you will stay." Joanne kissed her.

"Let's get back to the movie." Shanna rested her head on her shoulder. "Can we pause it for a minute?"

"Of course. You okay?"

"Yeah. I just thought of something." Shanna picked up her phone and typed a text. "I sent a text to the Realtor letting her know he has no right to bother her about the house sale."

"Good idea." Joanne restarted the movie.

Joanne smiled when Shanna began to sing "We're Off to See the Wizard." She put her arm around her and pulled her close. "I'm glad you're feeling better."

"I am. It's frustrating for me to know Paul is back from California. I'd hoped he was gone for good."

"At least he doesn't know where you live now, so he can't bug you."

"Yes!" Shanna blew out a breath.

"Before I forget, I scheduled the replacement of my carport for tomorrow. They'll be here by eight in the morning."

"I'll keep an eye out for them." Shanna hugged her. "Would you mind if I spent a little time sketching? It relaxes me."

"Not at all. Hopefully, it'll take your mind off Paul's text." She kissed Shanna and went to make herself a cup of tea. She made two cups and took one to Shanna.

"Thank you, honey." Shanna took a sip.

"I'm going to read for a while." Joanne changed into her pajamas and propped herself against her pillows in bed before losing herself in her book. She woke to soft kisses and the warmth of Shanna's body pressed against her. "Mm. Nice."

"Sorry to disturb your reading, but you looked so comfy and cozy I couldn't resist you."

"You can disturb me like that any time." Joanne pulled her closer. "Finished sketching the next masterpiece?"

"I am." Shanna propped herself on pillows next to her. "I feel more at peace with things."

"Good. You deserve to feel at peace."

"I can't figure out why he's back from California."

"Maybe he regrets leaving you?"

"I doubt it. More than likely his girlfriend kicked him out." Shanna rolled to her side and slid her arm over Joanne. "Am I interrupting your reading?"

"I'll take cuddling with you over reading any day." Joanne set her book aside and pulled Shanna on top of her.

❖

Joanne smiled when she pulled in behind Shanna's car in her new carport when she got home from work the next day. She followed a very enticing scent to the kitchen and lifted the lid on a pot of spaghetti.

"Hi, honey." Shanna hugged her from behind. "I made one of the three things I know how to cook. I can boil the noodles for it, too."

"Thanks for making it. Let's eat and then go shop for a bed."

"Okay. Do we have extra sheets and a blanket?"

"Oh. I guess I need to make a list."

"I'll remember. Just think of what you have on your bed."

"Pillows!" Joanne grinned.

"Yes. We'll get a couple."

Joanne helped Shanna empty her car when they returned from the shopping trip. "I'm glad they can deliver the mattress." She put away the pillows and bedding.

"Yes. It'll be here before Heather gets here." Shanna called out from the kitchen. "Are you expecting anyone? Someone just pulled into the driveway."

Joanne joined her in the kitchen. "Maybe it's someone turning around. That happens a lot here." She looked out the window. "No one's there now."

"Let's walk over to Mom's."

"Maybe we should call first." Joanne picked up her phone and called Betty. "She said to come on over. She'll have tea ready."

"I'm glad you called." Betty set two cups of tea on the coffee table. "How did the move go?"

"It went smoothly," Shanna said. "I have my house on the market and I hope it sells quickly."

"How is Mr. Levine, Betty?"

"He's doing well. Eileen and I had lunch the other day, and he was working in their shed."

"Good." Joanne relaxed as she sipped her tea. "It has to be scary for her. Heart attacks are terrifying."

"Yes. I understand every heart attack weakens the heart. The doctor told me that when Jim died. He died from only one." Betty wiped away a tear.

Joanne hurried to change the subject. "My friend Heather is coming to visit. You'll have to come over for dinner while she's here."

"I look forward to it. I'll bake a Bundt cake."

"That sounds perfect, Betty." Joanne hugged her. Joanne took Shanna's hand as they walked home. "I'm glad your mom lives so close to us. She's special."

"She is and I know she likes you a lot."

"Let's watch the news before bed." Joanne turned on the TV and settled next to Shanna on the couch. "Have I told you how glad I am that you're here with me?"

"Several times." Shanna kissed her. "I'm not going anywhere."

"I know." Joanne took her hand and cradled it in her lap. "We have a few more neighbors to help this week."

"I figured there would be." Shanna sighed. "Mom has the list of most needy. We can start tomorrow."

"Yes. Tomorrow. I'll be home by four thirty." Joanne put her feet up on the coffee table and wrapped her arm around Shanna. She relaxed in the knowledge Shanna was here with her and they could build a life together. She never believed growing up that she'd be able to have a normal life, much less have someone special to spend it with. Her teachers and her parents had prepared her for a life of difficulties. She wasn't expected to be able to hold down a job, live alone, or have a meaningful relationship with anyone. She'd accomplished all of that and now she had Shanna in her life. She looked forward to sharing all of that with Heather when she came to visit.

"Are you all right? You looked a little lost there for a minute," Shanna said.

"I am. I was just thinking about how much I have to be grateful for. You're at the top of my list."

"I'm happy about that." Shanna kissed her. "We all have things we can't do or understand, but I believe we also have the ability to concentrate on what we can do and make the most of that. Whatever we accomplish in life, is a reflection of how much effort we put into it. In my opinion anyway."

CHAPTER THIRTY-FOUR

S hanna rolled over and snuggled closer to Joanne. She loved to feel the heat of her body so close and the steady beat of her heart under her palm. A fierce protectiveness overcame her when she thought of Joanne's disorder. She couldn't protect her from the world, but she could support her and be available for whatever she needed. She drifted back to sleep and woke half an hour later alone.

"Morning, sleepy head." Joanne crawled back into bed and pulled her on top of her.

"Morning." Shanna kissed her and slid her hand between them.

"I have to get up. Work, remember?"

"I do." Shanna sighed. "You're mine later."

"All yours." Joanne kissed her and went to take a shower.

Shanna considered sneaking into the shower with her but decided she'd wait until they had more time. She prepared oatmeal for breakfast and set two bowls on the table.

Joanne came out of the bathroom wrapped in a towel. "Looks good. Thanks for making this." She kissed Shanna and finished her oatmeal before dressing. "I'll see you tonight."

Shanna washed the few breakfast dishes and went to finish a sketch she'd started the day before. She worked for an hour and when she went to refill her coffee cup, she glanced out the kitchen window just as a delivery truck pulled into the driveway.

She put the sheets, blanket, and pillows on after they set up the bed and stepped back to admire it. It was ready for their company. She sat and enjoyed the idea of them having company. She'd been a couple with Paul, but it was to keep her parents happy. She'd pretended for too many years and now she had the real thing. She could admit real feelings for Joanne. Exactly what they were she wasn't sure. Or did she not want to admit? Satisfied that the bed was ready for company, she turned to the latest manual her boss had sent her. She worked for the rest of the day and went to the refrigerator to decide on what to make for dinner. She decided on macaroni and cheese but smiled in surprise when Joanne came home with pizza. "Thanks for bringing pizza!"

"I thought it would be a nice change. And you wouldn't have to cook. You know, you don't have to do all the cooking. I'm no chef, but I can make a few things." Joanne pulled her into her arms and kissed her.

"Okay. You cook tomorrow."

Shanna set the table and put the pizza in the middle before sitting. "This is great. Easy and I love pizza."

"Me too." Joanne took a bite.

"How did work go today?" Shanna asked.

"It was fine. I'm getting to know many of the people with accounts there. It's nice they call me by name now."

"That's great. I'm glad it's working out for you."

"My doctor explained to me as a teen why I struggled with reading and arithmetic, but told me if I studied and applied myself I could hold down a job and make my way in the world. My parents were very proud of me when I got the job as a teller. I worked hard for it and I'm grateful for my boss's patience."

"I'm proud of you, too. I think many people in your position would've given up." Shanna kissed her.

"I almost did several times, but my parents' belief in me kept me going."

"They sound like special people. I'm sorry you lost them."

"I'm sorry they never had a chance to meet you. I'm certain they'd approve." Joanne finished her pizza and took their plates to the kitchen.

Shanna closed the now empty pizza box and took it to the garbage. "I like this easy clean-up."

"Wow. This room looks great." Joanne said from the extra bedroom. "Thanks for putting the bed together."

"It wasn't hard. They delivered it this morning."

"I think we should try it out." Joanne pulled her against herself and kissed her.

"Good idea." Shanna led her to the bed and lay on her back. "Join me?" She held out her hand and tugged her on top of her.

"It's going to be just fine." Joanne hugged her.

"Has Heather let you know when she'll be here?"

"Not yet. She has clients to reschedule."

"Okay. I have something I'd like to do in here, but I wanted to make sure you were okay with it."

"What do you have in mind?"

"I'd like to put a room divider here." She pointed to her and area by her desk. "To separate my work space from the sleeping area."

"That's a good idea. There's plenty of room."

"Great. I'll figure something out tomorrow. Mom called today. She's invited us for a visit tonight. Do you feel like going there for a while?"

"Sure. We haven't visited her lately."

"I think she's a little lonely."

"Then let's go." Joanne held Shanna's hand as they walked across the street.

"Come in, you two. I'm so glad you're here. I was beginning to think you forgot about me."

"Never!" Shanna and Joanne both hugged her.

"We've been busy settling in. My friend Heather is coming to visit so we set up the extra bedroom." Joanne settled on the couch with Shanna.

"And I've been busy working and hoping my house sells soon."

"How's that going?" Shanna's mom asked as she set cups of tea on the coffee table.

"It's been shown a few times, but no offers yet." Shanna didn't bother telling her mother about Paul's text objecting to the sale.

"Would you like to come over for dinner this week? I'll be cooking." Joanne sat up pretending to be very proud.

"I'd love to. Just say when."

"How's the neighborhood watch going? I was wondering if there were still neighbors that needed help," Joanne said.

"There are." Betty went to her bedroom and returned with a piece of paper. "These are the ones who are still waiting for help with cleanup. Many people still need carports replaced, too."

Joanne looked at Shanna. "Think we could help some more?"

"Probably cleaning up, but the carports have to be that company. We'll review your list, Mom. Hopefully we can help." Shanna sipped her tea.

"How's Mr. Levine doing?" Joanne asked.

"He's much better. He's been working in his shed and he replaced that broken window himself."

"Great. I'm glad he's doing so well."

"Do they ever come over for dinner?" Joanne asked.

"Before his health declined, they did. I hadn't thought about it, but maybe I'll invite them. I think they've isolated themselves since his heart attack."

"We could invite them along with you. Maybe they'd be more comfortable with you there."

"I think that's a great idea." Betty grinned.

"We should probably get home and let you relax," Shanna said.

"Yeah, and I have to be at work early tomorrow," Joanne mumbled.

"Thanks for coming over. I miss you two." Betty hugged them.

"That same car we saw earlier just pulled into our driveway and left again." Shanna tried to get the license plate number but couldn't. She made note of the brownish color and make. "Maybe we should let the police know about it. Maybe it's some kind of surveillance to check on when they can break into the house." She took a deep breath to settle her nerves. "I'm a little scared."

"Honey, it's probably just someone lost or looking for a specific address."

"Okay, but I'm going to call anyway." Shanna looked up the police number and called as soon as they got in the house. "They're going to send a patrol car through the neighborhood."

"Good. I hope you feel better." Joanne kissed her.

Shanna checked that all the windows and doors were locked before settling on the couch with Joanne. "You have to admit it's weird. We don't have cars turning in our driveway often."

"Not often," Joanne said. "But it doesn't mean it can't happen." She took Shanna's hand and kissed it. "I'll protect you." She grinned.

"I'm a little uneasy since Paul's text." She snuggled into Joanne's embrace.

"I get it, and I hope he stays out of your life."

"I think he will. Our marriage was a farce. It satisfied my parents' and his need to have a wife."

"Your mom wanted you married?"

"She and my dad hoped for me to marry and live happily ever after. They were pretty traditional and wanted to see me happy."

"Betty, your mom, seems okay with us being together."

"She is. She sees how happy I am now and regrets pushing me into marrying Paul. It feels good to be accepted by her now."

"I told you I was sixteen when I was adopted, so I'd already begun to recognize I was attracted to girls. I talked to my mother about it, and she told me they loved me and she and Dad wanted me to be happy and would support any choice I made. I like to think they're looking down at me from Heaven and are happy I found you."

"They probably are, honey. I'm going to make some tea. Can I bring you a cup?" Shanna kissed her quickly before standing.

"Yes. Thank you."

Shanna kept an eye on the driveway as she made their tea. She couldn't shake the feeling of foreboding, and it was giving her a stomachache. She shook it off and carried their cups to the living room.

"Thanks, honey." Joanne took a sip of her tea.

"Let's watch *Wheel of Fortune*," she said.

CHAPTER THIRTY-FIVE

Joanne cradled Shanna's hand in her lap while they watched TV and tried to project calm and safety. Shanna jumped at every noise from outside and kept glancing at the window. "We're safe in here, honey." She squeezed her hand.

"I know. I'm sorry I'm so uneasy. I can't seem to get Paul's text out of my mind. He has a lot of resources and can travel easily."

"Your house will sell soon and you'll be totally done with him." She sighed when Shanna cuddled closer to her.

"I hope you're right."

Joanne hoped so, too. She relaxed and enjoyed the feel of Shanna's warmth next to her. The late night news came on and she shifted so Shanna's head rested in her lap. She began to doze and jumped at the sound of a car horn in her carport. "What the...?" Shanna stood and raced to the door. "Damn it."

"What's going on?" Joanne opened the door and saw Paul glaring at them from his car while he leaned on the horn. She called 911 and hoped the police would arrive before Paul got away. She quickly took a picture of him in his car. She heard the sirens before the police cars arrived.

"What the hell, Shanna?" he yelled as he crawled out of his car. "You sold the house out from under me? Where am I supposed to stay when I'm not traveling?" He shouted louder and began to stomp toward the door.

Joanne stepped in front of Shanna and gently pushed her back. "You get off my property. You're not welcome here, and I will press charges of harassment and trespassing if you don't leave now."

Paul glanced at the police cars in the street and glared at her before turning and leaving.

"Let us know if he comes back," the officer said. "You did good calling because domestic disputes can get nasty. You ladies take care."

Joanne held Shanna as she cried. "It's okay, honey. He's gone."

"I'm so sorry, Jo. I can't believe he came all the way here. He must have gotten my address from the Realtor. Damn." Shanna began to pace as she called them. "I'm calling to let you know that someone in your office gave my new address to my ex-husband. I'm very upset by that and you need to review your privacy policy." She disconnected the call.

"It's okay. He's gone now."

"What if he comes back? I can't stay here. I can't put you in danger!" Shanna began to cry again.

"Honey. You saw how quickly the police got here." Joanne took a deep breath. "He probably won't bother you again."

Shanna plopped onto the couch. "I can't be sure. I'm scared." She broke down and began to cry again.

Joanne held her and rocked. "It'll be okay, sweetheart. We'll figure something out."

"I had no idea he'd care if I sold the house. His name has been off the deed since the divorce." Shanna wiped her eyes and blew her nose. She took a deep breath and let it out slowly. "I need to make a plan."

"We need to make a plan." Joanne kissed her.

"Honey, Paul is my problem."

"You don't get it, love. We are 'we' and that means together. Your problem is my problem. I will do whatever we need to do to get him out of your life."

"I don't want you hurt. If he drove all the way here to harass me, he must not have anywhere to stay, but he's a lawyer. I can't believe he couldn't afford to rent an apartment or house somewhere. I think he wants to get back at me for insisting on a divorce. I'm not sure why though. He was messing around with his new girlfriend way before we split." Shanna sniffled and blew her nose.

"Didn't you tell me he had a girlfriend?"

"Yeah. I don't know where she lives. I thought Paul moved to California to be with her, but who knows." Shanna tipped her head on the back of the couch. "I never told you the whole story about us. My parents were very traditional about marriage. They wanted me to be happily married to a man. Paul fit their idea of a 'good man' so he and I made an arraignment. We'd appease my parents and get married, but it was on paper only. We bought that house in South Carolina and lived together but rarely slept together." Shanna took a deep breath before continuing. "I agreed to play the committed wife and attend all his events with him, and he agreed that it was only for appearance sake. Anyway, he was always agreeable to the situation, so I'm not sure why he's pissed off now. I wouldn't think he'd care that I moved on. I thought he had, too."

Joanne pulled her into her arms. "I don't know much about men except to know my father was a good one. My parents wanted to see me happy and probably thought my FASD would prevent me from having a serious relationship with anyone, male or female. They were wrong." She hugged Shanna tighter. "I care about you a lot, and I'll be here to help with whatever you need."

"I think the first thing to do is to request help from the police. He won't be able to come near us without the police catching him. Maybe I need a restraining order."

"I'll call them first." Joanne started a list. "What next?"

"I don't know, honey. I just don't know." Shanna broke down and cried.

Joanne put her list aside and pulled Shanna into her arms. "It'll be okay. Let's get a couple of those cameras for the carport. I think they work connected to our phones. We can see who's there."

"Yes. That's a good idea." Shanna wiped her eyes.

"Do you feel like going to the store to help me pick them out?" Joanne assumed the store employee could help her, but she didn't want to leave Shanna alone.

"Could we go tomorrow morning? I doubt he'd come back tonight." Shanna looked exhausted.

"Of course, honey. We'll go first thing when they open." Joanne took her hand and kissed it. "Let's go to bed."

Joanne woke the next morning and made coffee before going back to bed to hold Shanna. She didn't know what the future held, but she knew she would do everything possible to keep her safe. "Coffee?" she asked when Shanna murmured and snuggled closer.

"Stay here." Shanna kissed her and got out of bed. She returned in five minutes carrying two cups of coffee.

"Coffee in bed. What a luxury. Thank you, love." Joanne sat up and sipped from her cup and was pleased when Shanna sat next to her with hers. "How do you feel this morning?"

"Better." She took a drink of coffee. "We'll pick up the cameras for the carport."

"Yes, we will. He may never come back. The police might have scared him." Joanne kissed her.

"I hope so."

Joanne sipped her coffee and enjoyed the luxury of lounging in bed with Shanna. "The store with the cameras doesn't open until nine." She set her cup on the nightstand and Shanna did the same. "We have time." She slid her leg over Shanna's, shifted on top of her, and kissed her. She woke half an hour later and stretched before getting up to join Shanna in the kitchen. She nuzzled her neck and sat at the table with a bowl of oatmeal. "Thanks for making this."

"We needed to fortify ourselves before shopping on a Saturday. Let's get this done." Shanna led the way out the door and drove them to the police station first to request they do a daily drive-by. The trip to the store took a little longer, but she picked out two cameras, one for each end of the carport. "Ready to go home and set these up?"

"Yes." Joanne read the directions while Shanna drove. "It looks a little complicated to me." She reread them and tried to clear her confusion.

"I'll take a look at them when we get home. It'll be okay." Shanna smiled.

"I'm sorry, honey. I can't seem to understand how these work." Joanne frowned but held back her tears.

"It's okay. We'll have plenty of time to figure them out when we get home."

Joanne held the ladder while Shanna mounted the cameras. "Thank you, honey. I hope we don't need to use them, but I feel better with them there."

"I do, too." Shanna climbed off the ladder and made sure both of their phones received images. "I think we're all set."

"Shall we invite ourselves over to Betty's for a cup of tea?"

"Good idea."

Joanne checked her phone for images from the new cameras before finding Shanna and following her across the street.

"I'm not going to tell Mom about Paul. It'll only worry her."

"Okay," Joanne said, but she wondered if Paul knew where Betty lived. "Does he know where your mom lives?"

"Oh, damn. He does. We were only here to visit once. Hopefully, he's forgotten."

"Maybe we should get her a couple of these cameras." Joanne checked the time. "We could probably be back in an hour."

"The store is open tomorrow. I'll go pick them up and install them for her then."

"I'd feel better about it. Let's go drop in on her."

"It's good to see you. Come in. I've got hot water. Tea for you two?" Betty said before she retrieved cups and teabags from the cupboard.

"Sounds good. Thank you." Joanne relaxed and enjoyed Betty's company. Tomorrow would be soon enough to worry about Paul.

CHAPTER THIRTY-SIX

Shanna rolled over, pulled Joanne close, and held back tears. Her feelings for Joanne went way beyond caring. She was in love with her and she believed Joanne felt the same. She sighed. It didn't matter. She had to keep her safe, and if it meant leaving, she'd have to somehow. She'd give the cameras time because maybe Paul wouldn't bother coming back. Hopefully, he'd move on or go back to his girlfriend. Maybe the police would scare him enough to keep him away.

"Honey, I can feel you thinking." Joanne sat up and pulled her into her arms. "What's the matter?"

"I'm just worried, you know?"

"About Paul showing up? We have that covered." She kissed her. "We'll be fine."

"I don't want you in danger. I don't trust him." She stroked her cheek.

"I don't either. That's why we have the police on alert."

"Yes, we do. And cameras." She forced a smile.

"Promise me something, love," Joanne said softly.

"Anything."

"If you decide to leave me, you'll let me know so I can go with you."

Shanna chuckled. "I think that's doable." Shanna surprised herself with the answer. It was a much better option than leaving

Joanne behind. Maybe they could make a life in another state. She gave up anymore heavy thinking and relaxed with Joanne in her arms.

"Are you going to put cameras up at your mom's today?"

"Yes."

"I'll make dinner then and expect you to come home to me."

"I will." Shanna grinned. "I have a new manual to work on, too."

"Invite your mom for dinner. I'll bake a whole chicken with carrots and potatoes, and make a salad."

"Great." Shanna kissed her and went to take a shower before going to her mother's. She knocked on her door to let her know she was there and found a ladder to begin mounting the cameras.

"Good morning, dear. I see you're already hard at work," Betty said.

"Hi, Mom. I am. I'll make sure they work before I leave."

"Thank you for doing that although I'm not sure they're necessary."

"I told you about Paul's visit. He's pissed off because I sold the house. As far as I knew, he was living in California. Anyway, you call the police if he shows up here."

She finished the installation and made sure her mother's phone displayed the view before going in for a cup of coffee and to invite her to dinner. "I have a new manual to edit, so I better get home. I'll see you later."

"Why do you have to work on Sunday?" her mother asked.

"I don't, but since I have it I thought I'd get it done."

"Okay. Thanks for putting up the cameras and I'll be over about five."

Shanna walked home and checked that her phone and Joanne's displayed the view in the carport. "I'm home," she called from the doorway. "Mom will be here about five."

"Sounds perfect," Joanne called from the kitchen.

"I'm going to walk down to the Levines'. Mom told me she needed some help moving some furniture."

"Okay. See you in a while," Joanne said.

Shanna moved the Levines' kitchen table across the room to the area Eileen pointed to. Then she went to the living room to move a recliner Mr. Levine wanted to face the TV. She accepted the cup of coffee she was offered and thanked them before leaving.

"I'm back," she called as she got home and went to the kitchen. "Hello?" Joanne must have gone out somewhere, but her car was still in the carport. She walked through the house and found a scribbled note on the kitchen counter. *See how you like something taken out from under you! P.* Shanna raced outside and looked for Joanne. She called out as she walked around the house. Joanne was nowhere to be seen. Joanne liked to go for walks so she hurried around the block.

She checked her phone several times and cringed at the recording of Paul holding Joanne in a choke hold as he dragged her out the door. On the off chance she'd managed to get away from him, she went to several neighbors to ask if they'd seen Joanne with no luck. She was gone.

She swallowed her rising panic and called the police. After identifying herself, she told them Paul had abducted Joanne. She showed them the note he'd left when they arrived and explained the situation. They questioned her as to where he could have taken her and she showed them the recording on her phone. She went inside the house and searched each room for the third time. She found Joanne's keys in the drawer where she usually kept them.

"Damn it, Paul. Where the hell did you take her?" Shanna had no idea where Paul would have taken Joanne, but she wouldn't put it past him to leave her somewhere in the woods or on the side of the road. She stopped her frantic search and sat to think rationally. He'd probably ask for something in return for her release. Maybe he would, but she doubted he'd hurt her. Paul had never been physically abusive, and his behavior now seemed out of character. She made a kidnapping report with the police and then went to her mother's.

"Hi, honey. Is everything all right? You look terrible." Her mother poured a cup of coffee for her.

"Thanks, Mom. It's not, actually. I think Paul has kidnapped Joanne."

"Oh my! Why would he do that? And what's he doing in Florida?"

Shanna sat on the couch with her mother and told her the whole story about him showing up angry because she'd sold the house 'out from under him.' "I presume he'll contact me. I don't understand his intention, and I can't believe he thinks he can get away with this. He's a lawyer! He has to know kidnapping is a felony. He'll go to jail for a long time."

Her mother patted her leg. "It'll be okay, honey. I'm sure he'll bring her back. He's probably just trying to scare you."

"I sure hope you're right, Mom, but it's a major felony to kidnap someone. I need to get back and meet the police when they get there." Shanna took a deep breath to keep from breaking down in tears.

"You care a lot about her, don't you?"

"I love her, Mom. A lot."

Her mother nodded. "Go meet the police." Shanna checked her phone several times as she walked home. If Joanne still had her phone, maybe she could send a message. Paul was an idiot but he wasn't stupid. He'd probably taken her phone away from her.

She retrieved her laptop when she got home and tried to distract herself by working. She managed to edit a few pages and put her work aside. She tried to figure out why Paul would've put himself in a position to be charged with a felony. He might've been hurt badly by his California girlfriend and decided to hurt his ex-wife. Or maybe he had a nervous breakdown over the sale of the house. She gave up trying to figure out his motives and began to pace. She took deep breaths to keep the panic away and picked up her phone. Maybe Joanne still had her phone. She sent a text telling her she was looking for her. Even if Paul had her phone he probably wouldn't think that an odd message. She turned the phone's volume to high and set it on the table next to her. However this all turned out, Paul would pay dearly.

It was dark when Shanna opened her eyes. She hadn't planned to fall asleep and she scrambled for her phone. There still was no message. She made sure it was fully charged and made herself a cup of chamomile tea. She turned on the TV and tried to watch whatever was on late at night. She muted the sound and made a plan for the morning. If Joanne wasn't returned by then, she'd call the police station first thing and every hour if needed to get a progress report. She would've gone out driving around aimlessly but was worried she'd miss her if Paul decided to bring her back. She fell back into a restless sleep.

The next morning, Shanna called her mother. "Hi, Mom. I have a request for you."

"Anything you need, honey."

"Paul still has Joanne. I'm hoping you can use your neighborhood watch thing to spread the word. Maybe somebody somewhere has seen them."

"I'll get on it. We have a phone chain of sixty people. We'll find her."

"Thank you, Mom." Shanna's next call was to Joanne's boss. She told him Joanne had become ill overnight and wouldn't be able to get to work.

Chapter Thirty-seven

Joanne opened one eye slightly to try to see where they were. Lying in the back seat of Paul's car didn't give her much of a vantage point. They could be in Texas for all she knew. She twisted to pull her phone out of the back pocket of her jeans. It was difficult to do with her hands tied. It amazed her that he hadn't checked for it. She read the text from Shanna and fumbled the phone back into her pocket. Hopefully, she'd get a chance to reply when he stopped for gas again. "Where are you taking me?" she yelled from the back seat for what felt like the hundredth time.

"We're almost there. Now shut up."

She wiggled her fingers to relieve the discomfort from having her hands tied together. She felt disoriented and confused. Why would he do this? What were his plans? She tried to stop the tears because she couldn't reach her face to wipe them away and hung on to memories of Shanna. Would she ever see her again? Would Paul leave her in this back seat to die? At least she'd managed to spit out the pill he'd forced into her mouth. She didn't know what it was but knew it could probably hurt her. He got back into the car after putting in gas. He surprised her by turning to look at her. "We're almost there. Keep your mouth shut and you might make it through this."

Joanne swallowed and clamped her teeth together. Maybe he didn't intend to kill her. She felt the car turn and presumed they were back on the expressway. She closed her eyes and prayed.

Joanne opened her eyes when the car jolted to a stop. She had no idea how long she'd slept or where they were. Her wrists were rubbed raw from the rope and all her joints ached from being cramped into the back seat.

"Get out," Paul yelled.

"I can't sit up." Joanne frowned in confusion. What was he doing now? She heard his door open and close and he grabbed her by the shoulders and pulled her out of the car and rolled her to the side of the road. She had no idea what road they were on or even what state they were in. She realized he'd loosened the ties on her hands and feet before he drove away so she managed to untie them and sit up. Tears gushed out when she saw he'd dropped her off at the end of her driveway. She slowly tried to stand but ended up on her hands and knees and fell to her side.

"Oh God. Honey, are you all right?" The sight of Shanna running toward her brought more tears.

"I am now." Joanne relaxed into her arms and stumbled up the driveway.

"The police need to talk to you to make a report. Are you feeling up to it now, or should I tell them to come back tomorrow?"

She clutched Shanna's hand and took a deep breath. "No, I want to get it over with." The officer wrote down all the information Joanne gave him and assured her the report would be filed immediately and they would conduct an intensive search for Paul. He'd be arrested for kidnapping and spend years in prison. She thanked the officer and prayed they'd be able to catch Paul soon. She followed Shanna to their bedroom and sighed with gratitude when she brought her a cup of Chamomile tea. She closed her eyes and woke an hour later in their bed next to Shanna who had her arm around her. She shifted closer and closed her eyes.

"You're home safe now, love." Shanna's voice filtered through her sleepiness.

Joanne startled awake half an hour later and looked for an escape route. She kicked her feet and moved her arms. She was no longer tied up in the back seat of a car. She stopped her thrashing and wrapped her arms around Shanna. "I'm sorry. I was so scared."

"I know, love. I was, too. I thought I'd lost you." Shanna held her tightly.

"Why did he do it?" Joanne asked but didn't expect an answer.

"I wish I knew. I think he went a little crazy when he found out the house was sold. I'm not sure why he'd care, but maybe his girlfriend kicked him out. I don't know, but he's being charged with kidnapping. When they catch him, he'll do jail time."

"He didn't hurt me. He had me tied up in the back seat of his car. I don't know where he took me, but he drove all night and then released me."

"I was so worried. He'll pay for this!" Shanna pulled her close.

"I'm home and I'm fine, honey. A little shaken, but he could have injured me. He tried to make me take a pill. I spit it out and don't know what it was. I just knew I probably shouldn't."

"So, he abducted you and tried to poison you! He's going to jail. The son of a bitch!" Shanna called the police to update their report.

"It's all right, love. I'm home and he's gone. I just realized I need to call my boss." Joanne hurried off the bed.

"I called him, honey. I told him you'd been ill overnight."

"Thanks. I'll be sure to get there a little early tomorrow."

She lay back on the bed and closed her eyes. She woke to the scent of chicken soup. She got up and followed the scent to the kitchen where she found Shanna stirring the pot of soup. "I made soup!" Shanna said.

"It smells yummy. Can we have some soon? The only thing I had to eat all night was potato chips. Paul stopped at a gas station and bought a bag for me. I'm ready for real food."

"I'll never forgive him for what he did to you. I can't shake off the anger and frustration."

Joanne pulled her into her arms. "I'm home and I'm fine. It was a scary event and I agree that he had no right to do what he did, but it's over. I'm safe." Joanne felt safe in Shanna's embrace. She knew the stress of the abduction would hit her and she'd be on the phone to Heather. For now, she'd try to relax and enjoy a good meal with Shanna.

"Let's invite your mom over tonight for a cup of tea." Joanne said.

"Good idea. I know she's worried about you."

"She knows, too?"

"Yes. I was frantic. I didn't know what to do, so I asked her to check with the neighbors to neighbors thing she does."

"She'll be happy to see I'm okay then." Joanne smiled, knowing Betty cared about her. She called Betty and smiled at her excitement. "I hope you can come over for a cup of tea tonight."

"She'll be over about six. Do you mind if I lie down for a little while?"

"Of course not. You go rest." Shanna kissed her.Joanne went to their bedroom and sat up on the bed to make a call to Heather. She answered on the first ring.

"Hi, Jo. Everything okay?"

"It is now. I had a bit of a scary event, and I need to talk about it."

"I'm glad you called. What happened?"

Joanne told Heather about being kidnapped and her terror at being tied and trapped in the back seat of his car for most of the night. She felt calmer after telling her story and doing deep breathing exercises. Heather confirmed the date she planned to visit and told her to call back if she needed to talk. "Thank you, Heather. I appreciate you being there to help me." She did a few more of her deep breathing exercises and fell asleep. A few minutes later, she felt the bed jiggle and the warmth of Shanna's hand in hers. She was home, she was safe, and she was loved. She closed her eyes and slept.

❖

Joanne rolled over and realized she was alone in the bed. She stretched and felt somewhat rested from her ordeal so she got up and changed. "Betty here yet?" she asked Shanna.

"Not yet. Did you have a good rest?"

"I did. I was more impacted by the whole thing than I thought. I can't figure out why he did it. What did he want from me? Was it just to scare you?"

Shanna showed her the note Paul had left. "I think he was telling me taking you away from me was like my sale of the house was taking it away from him and he wanted me to feel what he felt."

"He's an idiot. I hope he gets put in jail for the rest of his life!"

"Me, too. Honey. You were grabbed, tied up, and taken against your will. That's not something you can just shrug off. We'll have a nice evening with my mom and relax, but expect that you might have scary flashbacks."

"I'll try to relax, sweetheart." Joanne kept her focus on the many positives in her life. Most of all Shanna. She put the kettle of water on the stove to boil and snuggled next to Shanna to wait for Betty.

"Hello," Betty called from the door.

"Come on in, Mom."

"Hi, Betty." Joanne hugged her.

"Hey, Joanne. I heard about your ordeal. Are you okay?"

"Just shaken up some. Thanks, Betty. He didn't hurt me other than tying my hands and keeping me in the back seat of his car. I didn't know where we were or going. It was scary." Joanne took a deep breath and clenched her fists to keep her hands from shaking.

"I'm glad you're back and we're all having tea together."

"Me too. It feels familiar. It helps." Joanne toasted with her cup. "Are you doing well?"

"I am. The Levines still talk about how helpful you two were."

"Yeah? I'm glad. Shanna went to help them move some furniture yesterday just before…" Joanne's throat constricted and her heart raced at terrifying memories. "I'm sorry." She wiped away tears and gulped her tea.

Betty sat next to her on the couch and pulled her into a hug. "It'll be okay. The memories will fade with time."

"Thank you, Betty. I know they will." Joanne found the calm she'd acquired from talking to Heather and smiled. "It'll take a little time."

She listened to Betty talk about her neighbors' projects and the events she planned for the summer.

She snuggled closer to Shanna when she sat next to her. She had Betty on one side and Shanna on the other. She basked in the feeling of safety.

"That was a nice visit," Joanne said as she wound her arms around Shanna's neck.

"It was. I'm glad you enjoyed it and I hope it took your mind off bad memories for a while."

"It did, love. Thank you."

CHAPTER THIRTY-EIGHT

That's the last cup." Shanna set the cup in the drain board. "Let's go to bed."

She took Joanne's hand and led her to the bedroom noting how tired she looked despite her nap earlier. "How about a massage?" She opened a cupboard in the bedroom and retrieved her massage oil. "Lie face down on the bed and I'll start with your back." Shanna warmed the oil with her hands and began massaging Joanne's shoulders. She felt her begin to relax under her touch and moved to her back and arms. She poured more oil on her hands and continued down Joanne's body until she finished with her feet. She leaned and kissed her softly on her shoulder. "Feel better, baby?"

Joanne hummed and murmured quietly. "Thank you, love."

Shanna smiled and hoped she'd helped Joanne heal.

The next morning, Shanna got up with Joanne and scrambled eggs and made toast for them before Joanne had to leave for work.

"Thank you for making breakfast." Joanne kissed her.

"You're welcome. I'm glad you got some sleep last night. Are you sure you don't want to take today off? I'm sure your boss would understand."

"You helped a lot with that massage. I'm really pissed at Paul, but I feel calm about the whole thing. Where'd you learn to give massages?"

"I taught myself with a video. I thought I might start my own business one day doing it, but changed my mind when it was mostly men who wanted massages and more."

"You can practice on me any time you'd like." Joanne leaned on her against the counter top and kissed her. "I hope we have time tonight to continue this." She brushed her fingers over her breast and nuzzled her neck.

"Oh yes. Definitely." It was going to be a long day, Shanna thought.

After Joanne left for work, Shanna took an inventory of the refrigerator and cupboards and made a shopping list before going to the local grocery store. Neighbors waved at her as she pushed her cart up and down the aisles. She felt welcome and at home in this neighborhood. She loaded her car with bags of groceries and headed home. She turned onto their street and saw the same car they'd seen turning around in their driveway. "Damn." Was that Paul back again? She strained to see the driver but the car sped the opposite direction. She parked and unloaded the groceries before locking her car and the door to the house. They'd filed the kidnapping report so all she had to do was get the police here in time to catch Paul and he'd be taken into custody. She kept an eye on the camera feeds on her phone while she put the groceries away. It looked like he'd given up. If it had been Paul. She called the number the police had given her to use if Paul showed up again and reported sighting his car. A few minutes later, two police cruisers with lights flashing pulled up in front of the house. She described his car to the officers and told them which way he'd gone before thanking them for their swift response, going back into the house, and double-checking that all the doors were locked.

Shanna went to her work area and began edits on the latest manual she'd received while checking the street and driveway every ten minutes. She worked for a few hours and got up to make herself a cup of coffee. She automatically checked her phone for the camera feed and saw her car but nothing out of the ordinary. She planned on making lasagna for dinner so she set her phone alarm for four o'clock and went back to work. She hurried to the sound of breaking glass and checked the camera feed. Paul stood with a metal rod swinging at her car. The windshield was already smashed and he moved to the driver side window. "What the hell are you doing?" she yelled from the door and called 911. She feared going outside as Paul continued to smash the car windows and the hood. The police sirens grew closer and Paul paused for a second before continuing his rampage. He stood with the metal rod raised when the police arrived, so all three officers drew their weapons.

"Drop the rod," one of them yelled. "Drop it or we shoot."

Paul looked crazed. He dropped the rod, but before the officers could get to him he ran out the side of the carport.

Shanna went to the back window and watched as Paul raced across several lots and disappeared. The police followed him and within minutes three more police cars showed up and joined the chase.

Shanna watched for a few minutes and went to check the locks on all the windows and both doors. Paul was foolish if he thought he could get away, but she grabbed a kitchen knife and kept an eye on the direction he'd run. She went back to try to work on her manual but couldn't concentrate. She kept looking out the window fearing Paul would be back with that metal rod to use on her. She jumped at the loud knocking on the door. She hid behind a wall and peeked through the window expecting to see Paul. It was an officer and she breathed a sigh of relief.

"We got him, ma'am. He's the one responsible for the kidnapping is that correct?"

"Yes. He's the one who kidnapped my friend yesterday. He has a warrant out for his arrest. His name is Paul Mills. Felony kidnapping."

"Okay. He's locked in one of our cruisers and he's going to jail. Sorry for the scare. You take care." The officer tipped his hat and turned to leave.

"Thank you," she called out as he left the carport. Shanna plopped onto their couch and leaned her head back. She thought she probably had a small inkling of what Joanna had felt. Panic hadn't come close to describing what she felt when she saw him with the metal rod beating on her car. She couldn't imagine what had happened to him. She didn't remember a time he even lost his temper much less went crazy like he had.

Shanna gave up trying to work for the rest of the day. She swept the broken glass out of the carport and put it into the trash before using Joanne's shop-vac to vacuum the glass out of her car. She'd call her insurance company tomorrow. She put everything away and went to lie down. She woke to the feel of soft warm lips on hers and felt the bed move as Joanne lay next to her.

"What happened to your car, honey?"

Shanna pulled her close. "Paul did. He came back today for some reason. I guess to trash my car, I don't know."

"I'm so sorry. He's a scary guy."

"Well, he's finally in jail now."

Joanne sat up and stared at her. "Really?"

"Yes. The officer told me he'd be in jail tonight. I reminded him of his kidnapping charge but he already knew. They had a BOLO for him. I hope they put him in jail and throw away the key."

"Oh, me too, honey. But what's a BOLO?" Joanne kissed her.

"It stands for Be On the Lookout. I was going to make lasagna for dinner, but then all hell broke loose."

"I'll order a pizza. We can take my car to pick it up."

Shanna got up and followed Joanne to her car. "Isn't the pizza place an eat-in also?"

"Yeah. Let's do that."

Shanna plopped onto the couch when they got home and turned on the TV. "Let's watch *Jeopardy*. I don't even want to hear the news. I had enough news for one day."

"Okay with me. Would you like a cup of tea?" Joanne stood and went to the kitchen. She returned with two cups of chamomile tea.

Shanna sipped her tea as she leaned against Joanne. "This is nice."

"Yes, it is." Joanne rested her arm around Shanna and pulled her close. "I feel a huge relief to know Paul is in jail."

"I do, too, Jo. I can't figure out what happened to him. He was never like he was today. It was as if he was on drugs. Maybe he was."

"Maybe so. I told you he tried to make me take a blue pill. Maybe he got involved in drugs with that new girlfriend you told me about."

"Whatever happened to him has ruined his life." Shanna rested her head on Joanne's shoulder.

"It's eleven o'clock, sweetheart. Shall we go to bed?" Joanne stood and gently pulled Shanna off the couch.

"Mm. I was so cozy next to you."

"We'll get cozy in bed." Joanne led Shanna to their bedroom and helped her undress and put on her night shirt.

"Thank you. I think this event with Paul has taken a lot out of me. I was scared he would come after me with that metal rod. It was awful."

Shanna fought to stay awake until Joanne slid into bed next to her. She felt the warmth of her body and her arm holding her possessively as she drifted to sleep.

The next morning, Shanna rolled to her side, reached for Joanne, and sat up. The scent coming from the kitchen made her mouth water as she entered and sat at their small table. "Something smells yummy," she said.

"Morning, babe. Feel better this morning?" Joanne kissed her and went back to the stove.

"I do and whatever you're cooking smells wonderful." She poured a cup of coffee and rested her hand on Joanne's back.

"It's an omelet." Joanne looked proud of herself. "Heather taught me how to make these and I wanted to surprise you. I hope you're feeling more settled after Paul's idiocy."

Shanna put her coffee on the table and set it with plates and silverware before sitting. Joanne placed an omelet on each plate and sat across from her. "I am. I just don't know what happened to him to make him go nuts."

Joanne hurried to the refrigerator and poured two glasses of juice. "One for you and one for me." She sat and took a bite of her omelet. "Who knows, but he's in big trouble if he ever comes back."

"You're right about that. I'll make sure he's charged with a felony to keep him in jail forever! This is a wonderful breakfast, honey. Thanks for doing it." Shanna took a drink of coffee and a bite of omelet. "Yep. You can cook anytime you want to."

CHAPTER THIRTY-NINE

Joanne dressed for work and wished she could stay home and hold Shanna all day. She was aware that her overprotectiveness stemmed from the traumatic events caused by Paul. But, he was in jail and they were safe. She'd spoken to Heather several times when she'd come for a visit and felt more settled than she had. Heather had suggested she and Shanna see a counselor, so they made an appointment with a woman in a local practice.

"I'll see you tonight, love." She kissed Shanna and went to work. The day dragged for her and she had to keep pushing aside thoughts of their meeting with the counselor that evening. She was used to talking to Heather, but their counselor was a new person in her life and she hesitated talking to her about personal things. She finished her workday and went home.

"I'm home, love." She found Shanna at her drafting table working. She pulled her into her arms and kissed her. "I'd like to talk tonight."

"Me, too. Let's pour glasses of your sparkling cider and sit in the living room." Shanna took her hand and led her to the couch. "You go first."

Joanne squeezed her hand gently and let go. "I'm uncomfortable...no. I don't think...well, I don't want to see this new counselor anymore. I'm not comfortable with her. Maybe I've

been spoiled by Heather, but I get the impression she's not interested in what we have to say."

"Oh, honey. I know what you mean. I'm not happy with her
either. I'd hoped she'd be more helpful once she got to know us,
but I get the impression she's just listening because she's being
paid to."

"Do you think we need one? A counselor, I mean."

"It probably can't hurt. I know I still have bad dreams about
the whole mess. I wish Heather were closer."

"Yeah, me too." Joanne considered an option. "Have you ever
used Zoom?"

"I have. Are you thinking Heather might be willing to?"

"I'm going to ask her if you'd like to try it." Joanne suppressed
her excitement waiting for Shanna's answer.

"Let's contact her tonight."

Joanne called Heather and left a message when she got her
voice mail. "She'll call back," she told Shanna.

The phone rang within ten minutes. "Hello, Heather. Thank
you for calling back. Shanna and I aren't comfortable with our
counselor and would like to know if you'd be willing to work with
us." Joanne took a breath. "We thought we could do it over Zoom.
Okay, thank you, Heather."

"She'll check her schedule and get back to us tonight," Joanne
told Shanna.

"Great. I hope she's available." Shanna pulled her into her
arms and kissed her. "I feel a little better about the ordeal. I think,
in time, we'll heal and I won't jump at every strange car that slows
as it goes by."

"I do, too and I trust Heather to guide us if we get off track."

Joanne pulled Shanna into her arms and kissed her. "I love
you, you know."

"Oh, honey. I love you, too. We're going to heal from this and
make a peaceful life for ourselves."

"Yes, we are." Joanne's phone rang. "It's Heather." She
listened for a few minutes and grinned ear to ear. "We have an
appointment on Zoom Wednesday at seven p.m."

Joanne rolled on top of Shanna and kissed her while she slowly fondled her clit. She slid her finger into her warmth and stroked through her wetness. She loved feeling Shanna's slow build up to orgasm. She arched into her touch and moaned as she climbed closer to release. "That's it, love. Come for me." Shanna pressed her hands against hers and shuddered as she came. "Oh my. I love what you do to me." Shanna pulled her closer and kissed her.

"I could stay in bed all day and do that, but aren't we picking up your new car today?" Joanne asked.

"Yes. In a minute."

Joanne grinned when Shanna reversed their positions and rolled on top of her. She was wet and ready from making love to Shanna and she came the minute Shanna touched her.

"See. I knew it wouldn't take more than a minute."

Joanne held Shanna until her own breathing became normal. It wouldn't be so bad to stay in bed all day, but Shanna was looking forward to getting a car. Her trashed one was towed away days ago. "Let's go get your car so we can come back and do this all again."

❖

Joanne watched Shanna familiarize herself with her new car. It was smaller than her old one and brand new. "I like it." She smiled.

"Good. You deserve a new car." Joanne didn't add details of what happened to her old one. They were making good progress on therapy and putting the bad memories behind them. "I'll meet you at home." She drove home and grinned when Shanna pulled into the carport behind her.

"It rides so nice!" Shanna giggled. "You want to go for a ride?"

"Absolutely." Joanne climbed into the passenger seat and buckled her seat belt.

"I love it." Shanna gushed when they got home.

"It is a nice car." Joanne held her hand as they walked into the house.

"I'll pull it up front when you go to work tomorrow."

"Sounds good." Joanne pulled her into her arms and kissed her.

"What was that for?"

"Because I love you and like seeing you happy."

"I love you, too. Want to go for a ride with me tomorrow? I'd like to drive to the coast and watch the water for a while."

"Let's pack food and wade on the shore as soon as I get home." Joanne missed the water. They'd been so busy with life, they hadn't taken the time to just relax.

"Perfect." Shanna stepped out of her new car and wiped fingerprints off the door handle.

Joanne kept watching the clock all day at work. She looked forward to being by the water with Shanna.

Joanne pulled into the driveway when she got home and was surprised that Shanna's car wasn't there. She left room for Shanna to pull past her to get to the carport. She went into the house and began to gather food for their picnic by the water.

Shanna pulled in ten minutes later. "Sorry, love. I took my mom for a ride in my new car."

"No problem. I was just figuring out what to take with us."

"Peanut butter sandwiches would be fine with me."

Joanne shrugged. "Okay." She made four sandwiches, wrapped them in foil, and put them in a paper bag along with two bottles of water. "All set." She settled into the passenger seat of Shanna's new car and watched her carefully maneuver through traffic to get to the beach. They parked and set up lawn chairs to face the water. "This is a nice spot."

"It is." Joanne rested her arm around Shanna's shoulders. "Shall we have a sandwich?" She retrieved two from the bag and handed one to Shanna along with a bottle of water. "I love the sound of the waves on shore. I used to go to the shore of Lake Superior in Michigan and sit for hours reading and watching the water."

"It sounds nice. Do you miss living there?" Shanna asked.

"I miss my parents, but after they died there wasn't anything there for me." Joanne caught movement out of the corner of her eye. "It can't be!" She stood and pointed to a man standing a few yards away. "Shanna look!""Damn, it looks like Paul but it can't be. He's in federal prison. It's just a guy who looks a little like him." Joanne took a deep breath to quell the rising panic.

"Yeah. I see that now. I'm scared, honey. Am I going to see him everywhere now?" Joanne looked up and down the shore expecting to see Paul everywhere.

Shanna rested her head on her shoulder and Joanne pulled her close. "You're still reacting to the trauma. Remember what Heather told you. It will lessen in time. You'll feel safe again. We both will." She glanced at her phone to check the feed from the cameras.

Joanne stood, pulled Shanna up to stand next to her, and wrapped her arms around her. "We'll figure something out. I hate guns. They scare me, but hunting is a big thing in the upper peninsula of Michigan. My father didn't hunt, but he shot skeet. One day he took me to the range with him and taught me how to shoot a shotgun. I wouldn't be opposed to getting one for us."

Chapter Forty

Shanna was quiet for a long time. "So, you know how to shoot?"

"Only a shotgun. It's pretty much point and pull the trigger. If nothing else, I think it would scare anyone away."

"Will you show me how?"

"Yes. We'll go shop tomorrow."

"Okay. I'm so scared."

"A convicted felon won't be released from jail." Joanne called the number Shanna had for the police.

"Hello. My name is Joanne Billings and I was abducted by Paul Mills. I need to know that he will never be released from jail."

Shanna went to the kitchen and returned with two cups of tea. "Here. Tea is the answer to all our problems." She smiled.

Shanna sat on the couch. "Would you hold me? Please?" Joanne hurried to her side and pulled her into her arms. "I'm so angry at him. And scared. I still want to get that shotgun."

"We will. And maybe we can help your mom with that neighbor to neighbor thing she has working. They'd call the police if any of them see him."

"Are you okay, honey? You look tired."

Joanne sat up. "I am a little but I'm okay."

Shanna began crying again. "This is awful. I'm so sorry, love."

"It's not your fault. It's all him. I'm going to check on our cars."

Shanna followed her to the carport. Her new car sat quietly undisturbed. "If he touches my new car, I'll shoot him with that shotgun we're getting."

"Maybe just scare him with it. I don't want to have to try to get you out of jail for murder."

"Okay." Shanna went to the kitchen and refilled their cups of tea. "Let's watch *Jeopardy* again." She settled on the couch and pulled Joanne into her arms. "You drink your tea and rest. I love you."

"I love you, too," Joanne mumbled and fell asleep in her arms.

Shanna held her close and vowed to get them out of this Paul mess. She gently slid a pillow under Joanne's head and went to check the carport. She'd checked the camera feed but worried he might try to hide under or behind one of the cars. She grabbed a knife and carried it with her. She looked under the cars and walked around them. It looked clear so she went back into the house and locked the door. She settled on the couch and her phone rang. "Hi Mom."

"Hi, honey. I have a question for you. I know I met Paul years ago, but is he about five foot eight, dark hair, average build?"

"Yes, he is. Have you seen him?" Shanna felt panic bubbling.

"I didn't mean to scare you. I think one of the neighbors saw him creeping around."

"Please call the police if anyone sees him. He's a convicted felon. It may not be him, though. We saw a man on the beach that looked like him and got scared. It was just someone looking like him. We talked to the police and they told us he's in federal prison and he's not getting out."

Shanna gathered Joanne in her arms and watched TV while keeping an eye on her phone. She knew Paul was in prison but she still imagined she saw him. She shook herself a couple of times when she began to doze off. Joanne must have felt her tension rise because she sat up and took her hand. "You okay?"

"Yes. I talked to Mom and one of her neighbors thinks they saw Paul lurking around their house. I know it isn't him, but I still get nervous. I hope we can relax and feel safe again soon."

"Sorry I fell asleep on you." Joanne rubbed her face. 'I'll go check the carport." Joanne went to the carport and Shanna made them another cup of tea. It would either calm them or distract them by so many bathroom breaks. She startled by loud noises coming from outside and hurried out to the carport.

Joanne held out her hand and pulled her close. "This is amazing." She pointed to the street.

Shanna blinked and broke into laughter. A mass of people moved down the street like a swarm of locusts carrying shovels, rakes, brooms, and other yard utensils. "That bad man ever comes back here, he'll have hell to pay!" the leader of the group spoke when they stopped at the end of Joanne's driveway.

"That's for sure, but he probably won't mess with the neighbors helping neighbors group."

Betty rushed up the driveway and hugged Joanne then grabbed Shanna and hugged her. "I'm so glad you two are all right."

"We are thanks to you and your group."

"No, honey. It's our group. You two are part of us now and neighbors help each other." Her mother opened her arms and hugged Shanna and Joanne.

"Oh. Sweetheart, we have to buy more teacups!" Joanne said.

Shanna watched the group slowly disperse after she and Joanne thanked them individually and promised to attend the next neighborhood bar-b-que.

"I'll head home and leave you two to recover," her mother said.

"Will you join us for a cup of coffee or tea?" Joanne asked.

"Thank you, dear. I'd like that."

Shanna sighed in relief as she sipped her coffee and enjoyed her mother's company. Paul would spend the rest of his life in prison. She hoped.

"You two can relax now," her mother said.

"I hope so, Mom. I think it'll take me time to believe he's really gone forever." Shanna took Joanne's hand and squeezed gently. "I'm so sorry he managed to find us and disrupt our life."

"He's gone now, love." Joanne leaned against her side. "Let's talk to Heather this afternoon."

"You two get some rest. I'm right across the street if you need anything."

"Thank you, Betty," Joanne said as she stood to hug her.

"Yeah. Thanks, mom."

"Do you want to contact Heather now or wait until tonight?" Joanne asked when they went into the house.

"I'm exhausted. Let's do it tonight."

Joanne took her hand and pulled her to the bed. "A nap sounds like a good idea."

Shanna tried deep breathing and meditation to relax. Her mind raced with memories of Paul's sneer and threatening glare. Why did she ever marry him? Her attempt to appease her parents led her to choose him and force herself to pretend she was content, if not happy. She enjoyed the heat from Joanne next to her and knew in her heart this was her destiny. This was where she belonged. She snuggled closer and pulled Joanne closer.

"Are you okay, honey?" Joanne mumbled.

"I am. I'm so glad Paul's finally in prison, but I'm afraid it might take me awhile to settle down after all the stress."

"I hope I can help with that." Joanne rolled on top of her and kissed her.

"You feel so good." Shanna couldn't stop her tears as she held Joanne tightly.

"I hope those are happy tears, love."

"Happy, content, relieved, I love you tears." Shanna sighed. "We're free."

Epilogue

Joanne pulled into their carport and parked behind Shanna's car. She sighed deeply as she stepped out of her car and enjoyed the feeling of relief that she'd never have to worry about Paul lurking in the shadows. She and Shanna had spent the three weeks after his arrest working with Heather and healing from the traumatic ordeal. She still declined to ride in the back seat of a car if possible, but vowed to work on her fear. She knew it would take time before she could give up her daily scrutiny of the carport but considered every day she refrained from checking every corner and underneath their cars a positive step forward.

"Mmm, something smells delicious," she said as she sniffed the air in the kitchen. Shanna had begun to focus on cooking as a form of therapy and the aroma of tonight's meal hinted at one of her best endeavors. She kissed her before heading to the bedroom to change out of her work clothes. She wrapped her arms around Shanna from behind and whispered "I love you" when she returned to the kitchen to set their two-seater kitchen table. "So, what culinary delight have you created for tonight?"

"It's sausage jambalaya," Shanna said as she turned and kissed her. "It has smoked sausage, onions, bell peppers, celery, and garlic. Plus other stuff and seasoning."

Joanne filled two water glasses with ice water and set them on the table. "I still check under the cars every day," Joanne declared.

"It's okay, love. I still never go anywhere without watching the cameras on my phone. It'll take time."

"I called again today." Joanne took a deep breath and expelled it.

"He's still there, I presume."

"Yep. I wish I could let it go and believe he's rotting in jail for twenty years without feeling the need to check."

"He is, love. They've got him locked up in prison and we're healing."

❖

Shanna loaded the dishwasher while Joanne cleared the table after dinner. Her fear of Paul's return nagged at her despite her confidence that he was locked away. She went to her drafting table where she'd left the unopened letter. Her stomach churned with uncertainty as she picked it up and carried it to the couch where Joanne sat. "I got this in the mail today." She handed the envelope to Joanne.

"Huh. I would've thought he couldn't have any contact with you." She turned the envelope over in her hand and gave it back to Shanna.

"Yeah. I was surprised to get it." She willed her hands not to shake as she opened the envelope, pulled out the handwritten note, and began to read.

Dear Shanna. I was allowed to write this and I'm told it might give you some closure. I don't care if it does or doesn't and it's not an apology for my behavior. You're just like all the other women I've known. You move on and leave me behind. I don't regret anything I did except not tossing that dyke lover of yours into the ocean! Paul.

"Wow. He's an angry man."

"Yeah. I had no idea he could be so vitriolic. When we married, he agreed to the charade of our relationship, but I don't understand what happened. He told me he had someone else but maybe she left him and he went off the rails." Shanna stood and put the letter away in case the police wanted to see it. "Let's watch that comedy again tonight," Shanna suggested.

"Sounds good." Joanne turned on the TV and settled on the couch. "Would you like to go on a mini-vacation? Maybe to Disney World?"

"That might be just what we need! Let's plan it for a long weekend." Shanna smiled with happiness for the first time since their Paul experience. "Let me know when and I'll start packing."

About the Author

C.A. Popovich is a hopeless romantic. She writes sweet, sensual romances that usually include horses, dogs, and cats. Her main characters—and their loving pets—don't get killed and always end up with happily-ever-after love. She is a Michigan native, writes full-time, and tries to get to as many Bold Strokes Books events as she can. She loves feedback from readers.

Books Available from Bold Strokes Books

All This Time by Sage Donnell. Erin and Jodi share a complicated past, but a very different present. Will they ever be able to make a future together work? (978-1-63679-622-2)

Crossing Bridges by Chelsey Lynford. When a one-night stand between a snowboard instructor and a business executive becomes more, one has to overcome her past, while the other must let go of her planned future. (978-1-63679-646-8)

Dancing Toward Stardust by Julia Underwood. Age has nothing to do with becoming the person you were meant to be, taking a chance, and finding love. (978-1-63679-588-1)

Evacuation to Love by CA Popovich. As a hurricane rips through Florida, so too are Joanne and Shanna's lives upended. It'll take a force of nature to show them the love it takes to rebuild. (978-1-63679-493-8)

Lean in to Love by Catherine Lane. Will badly behaving celebrities, erotic sex tapes, and steamy scandals prevent Rory and Ellis from leaning in to love? (978-1-63679-582-9)

Searching for Someday by Renee Roman. For loner Rayne Thomas, her only goal for working out is to build her confidence, but Maggie Flanders has another idea, and neither are prepared for the outcome. (978-1-63679-568-3)

The Romance Lovers Book Club by MA Binfield and Toni Logan. After their book club reads a romance about an American tourist falling in love with an English princess, Harper and her best friend, Alice, book an impulsive trip to London hoping they'll each fall for the women of their dreams. (978-1-63679-501-0)

Truly Home by J.J. Hale. Ruth and Olivia discover home is more than a four-letter word. (978-1-63679-579-9)

View from the Top by Morgan Adams. When it comes to love, sometimes the higher you climb, the harder you fall. (978-1-63679-604-8)

Blood Rage by Ileandra Young. A stolen artifact, a family in the dark, an entire city on edge. Can SPEAR agent Danika Karson juggle all three over a weekend with the "in-laws," while an unknown, malevolent entity lies in wait upon her very skin? (978-1-63679-539-3)

Ghost Town by R.E. Ward. Blair Wyndon and Leif Henderson are set to prove ghosts exist when the mystery suddenly turns deadly. Someone or something else is in Masonville, and if they don't find a way to escape, they might never leave. (978-1-63679-523-2)

Good Christian Girls by Elizabeth Bradshaw. In this heartfelt coming of age lesbian romance, Lacey and Jo help each other untangle who they are from who everyone says they're supposed to be. (978-1-63679-555-3)

Guide Us Home by CF Frizzell and Jesse J. Thoma. When acquisition of an abandoned lighthouse pits ambitious competitors Nancy and Sam against each other, it takes a WWII tale of two brave women to make them see the light. (978-1-63679-533-1)

Lost Harbor by Kimberly Cooper Griffin. For Alice and Bridget's love to survive, they must find a way to reconcile the most important passions in their lives—devotion to the church and each other. (978-1-63679-463-1)

Never a Bridesmaid by Spencer Greene. As her sister's wedding gets closer, Jessica finds that her hatred for the maid of honor is a bit more complicated than she thought. Could it be something more than hatred? (978-1-63679-559-1)

The Rewind by Nicole Stiling. For police detective Cami Lyons and crime reporter Alicia Flynn, some choices break hearts. Others leave a body count. (978-1-63679-572-0)

Turning Point by Cathy Dunnell. When Asha and her former high school bully Jody struggle to deny their growing attraction, can they move forward without going back? (978-1-63679-549-2)

When Tomorrow Comes by D. Jackson Leigh. Teague Maxwell, convinced she will die before she turns 41, hires animal rescue owner Baye Cobb to rehome her extensive menagerie. (978-1-63679-557-7)

You Had Me at Merlot by Melissa Brayden. Leighton and Jamie have all the ingredients to turn their attraction into love, but it's a recipe for disaster. (978-1-63679-543-0)

All Things Beautiful by Alaina Erdell. Casey Norford only planned to learn to paint like her mentor, Leighton Vaughn, not sleep with her. (978-1-63679-479-2)

Appalachian Awakening by Nance Sparks. The more Amber's and Leslie's paths cross, the more this hike of a lifetime begins to look like a love of a lifetime. (978-1-63679-527-0)

Dreamer by Kris Bryant. When life seems to be too good to be true and love is within reach, Sawyer and Macey discover the truth about the town of Ladybug Junction, and the cold light of reality tests the hearts of these dreamers. (978-1-63679-378-8)

Eyes on Her by Eden Darry. When increasingly violent acts of sabotage threaten to derail the opening of her glamping business, Callie Pope is sure her ex, Jules, has something to do with it. But Jules is dead...isn't she? (978-1-63679-214-9)

Head Over Heelflip by Sander Santiago. To secure the biggest prizes at the Colorado Amateur Street Sports Tour, Thomas Jefferson will do almost anything, even marrying his best friend and crush—Arturo "Uno" Ortiz. (978-1-63679-489-1)

Letters from Sarah by Joy Argento. A simple mistake brought them together, but Sarah must release past love to create a future with Lindsey she never dreamed possible. (978-1-63679-509-6)

Lost in the Wild by Kadyan. When their plane crash-lands, Allison and Mike face hunger, cold, a terrifying encounter with a bear, and feelings for each other neither expects. (978-1-63679-545-4)

Not Just Friends by Jordan Meadows. A tragedy leaves Jen struggling to figure out who she is and what is important to her. (978-1-63679-517-1)

Of Auras and Shadows by Jennifer Karter. Eryn and Rina's unexpected love may be exactly what the Community needs to heal the rot that comes not from the fetid Dark Lands that surround the Community but from within. (978-1-63679-541-6)

The Secret Duchess by Jane Walsh. A determined widow defies a duke and falls in love with a fashionable spinster in a fight for her rightful home. (978-1-63679-519-5)

Winter's Spell by Ursula Klein. When former college roommates reunite at a wedding in Provincetown, sparks fly, but can they find true love when evil sirens and trickster mermaids get in the way? (978-1-63679-503-4)

Coasting and Crashing by Ana Hartnett Reichardt. Life comes easy to Emma Wilson until Lake Palmer shows up at Alder University and derails her every plan. (978-1-63679-511-9)

Every Beat of Her Heart by KC Richardson. Piper and Gillian have their own fears about falling in love, but will they be able to overcome those feelings once they learn each other's secrets? (978-1-63679-515-7)

Grave Consequences by Sandra Barret. A decade after necromancy became licensed and legalized, can Tamar and Maddy overcome the lingering prejudice against their kind and their growing attraction to each other to uncover a plot that threatens both their lives? (978-1-63679-467-9)

Haunted by Myth by Barbara Ann Wright. When ghost-hunter Chloe seeks an answer to the current spectral epidemic, all clues point to one very famous face: Helen of Troy, whose motives are more complicated than history suggests and whose charms few can resist. (978-1-63679-461-7)

Invisible by Anna Larner. When medical school dropout Phoebe Frink falls for the shy costume shop assistant Violet Unwin, everything about their love feels certain, but can the same be said about their future? (978-1-63679-469-3)

Like They Do in the Movies by Nan Campbell. Celebrity gossip writer Fran Underhill becomes Chelsea Cartwright's personal assistant with the aim of taking the popular actress down, but neither of them anticipates the clash of their attraction. (978-1-63679-525-6)

Limelight by Gun Brooke. Liberty Bell and Palmer Elliston loathe each other. They clash every week on the hottest new TV show, until Liberty starts to sing and the impossible happens. (978-1-63679-192-0)

Playing with Matches by Georgia Beers. To help save Cori's store and help Liz survive her ex's wedding they strike a deal: a fake relationship, but just for one week. There's no way this will turn into the real deal. (978-1-63679-507-2)

The Memories of Marlie Rose by Morgan Lee Miller. Broadway legend Marlie Rose undergoes a procedure to erase all of her unwanted memories, but as she starts regretting her decision, she discovers that the only person who could help is the love she's trying to forget. (978-1-63679-347-4)

The Murders at Sugar Mill Farm by Ronica Black. A serial killer is on the loose in southern Louisiana and it's up to three women to solve the case while carefully dancing around feelings for each other. (978-1-63679-455-6)

Fire in the Sky by Radclyffe and Julie Cannon. Two women from different worlds have nothing in common and every reason to wish they'd never met—except for the attraction neither can deny. (978-1-63679-573-7)